ROCK AND ROLL REFORM SCHOOL ZOMBIES

BRYAN SMITH

deadite
press

205 NE BRYANT
PORTLAND, OR 97211

AN ERASERHEAD PRESS COMPANY
WWW.ERASERHEADPRESS.COM

ISBN: 1-936383-27-6

Printed in the USA.

"There's nothing on the radio when you're dead."
—The Cramps

One
On Through the Night

November 17th, 1987

Rain slashed across the darkening sky. A brilliant flash of lightning followed a violent crash of thunder. The sizzling jolt forked before striking the ground, two white slashes on the turbulent horizon. To Wayne Devereaux, it looked as if God Himself was waging war against the earth. The hard drum of rain against the top of his Jeep Cherokee sounded like the relentless pop-pop-pop of automatic weapons fire on a battlefield. Not that he would have firsthand knowledge of how such a thing would sound. This was the late 1980's. Wide-scale armed conflicts spread across blood-drenched battlefields and continents were a thing of the past. There might well be war again, but it'd be America and the USSR tossing warheads at each other, and that'd be all she wrote for the human race.

But he'd seen Platoon and Full Metal Jacket numerous times. And the gun battles in those movies did sound eerily similar to what he was hearing now. He imagined himself as an MP speeding through the streets of war-torn Saigon as the North Vietnamese closed in on the city in the last days before the fall. The crack and boom of thunder morphed in his head becoming the sound of heavy artillery fire.

He imagined the wailing strains of a Hendrix tune. Massive guitar riff like the cry of a god. All the good 'Nam movies had Hendrix tunes out the ass. Jimi or the Doors. Wayne's taste in music ran more toward more modern stuff. Metal and glam. Some punk. Guns N' Roses and Faster Pussycat. Motorhead and the Sex Pistols.

The Cult. But yeah, he could really groove on some Hendrix right now. That and a toke or two from the ganja Steve Wade had on him would really complete the illusion.

Then the Cherokee's headlights picked out a large sign looming on the right.

The 'Nam fantasy flew apart as he sat up straight behind the steering wheel. He slapped Steve on the arm and said, "Yo, check it out. We're here."

Steve groaned and shook his head. His eyes fluttered open and he leaned forward, squinting at the sign. "Yeah. That's it, man." He produced a half-pint bottle of Southern Comfort from an inner pocket of his denim jacket and spun the cap off the bottle. "Fucking place looks creepy as hell. How the fuck we supposed to get her out of there?"

The big white sign read: SOUTHERN ILLINOIS MUSIC RE-EDUCATION CENTER.

Below that was a number to call for appointments.

Reading the sign sent a shiver up Wayne's spine. Demand was so high that many of these institutions had long waiting lists. Places like the SIMRC claimed to be able to "de-metal" teenagers. Kids would have their love for metal purged from their minds and have their spirits cleansed of the music's evil taint. Three or six months later (depending on program and institution), they would "graduate" and reenter the world, presumably ready to begin a long, bland existence as a contributing, productive member of society. A few of Wayne's friends had gone through these programs. They went in as sullen and defiant rebels and emerged as clean-cut, fresh-scrubbed little robots in preppy clothes. Piercings gone and tattoos covered. Long hair shorn. And when they talked they parroted the teachings of the re-education programs. It was like listening to flesh-and-blood tape recorders. Fucking creepy.

Wayne was lucky. His parents weren't rock and roll-hating fundamentalists. They had their own quirks and ways he didn't understand, but they were tolerable. Religious, but not in a zealous way. He thanked God for that every day.

His girlfriend hadn't been as lucky.

Hell, that was an understatement of fucking epic proportions. Melissa's mother was churchgoer and a drunken hypocrite, but her stepfather was the real problem. He was an evil, abusive bastard. Lucas Campbell liked to quote the bible and rant about liberals. And, of course, he condemned nearly all of Melissa's lifestyle choices, especially her interest in "devil music." So Wayne had been unsurprised when Lucas and Melissa's all-too-compliant drunk-ass mother shipped her off to the SIMRC at the beginning of the school year. Pissed off like a motherfucker, but unsurprised. And, of course, he had been utterly powerless he'd felt to do anything about it. Melissa was a minor. Her mother had the legal right to send her to the SIMRC, which Ronnie Raygun's administration viewed as a perfectly acceptable kind of "alternative school." There had been nothing Wayne could do about it.

Or so he'd thought.

The call had come in last night, waking him up at midnight. His dad knocked on his door and told him in a groggy voice that Melissa was on the phone and wanted to talk to him. Wayne leaped from the bed, pulled on boxer shorts, opened the door, and brushed past his bewildered father. He picked up the kitchen extension and said, "Melissa? Dad said—"

And then he heard the sound that nearly made his heart stop. That sniffle. A world of heartache resonated within that sound. Then she was talking, her voice low and shaky. "Wayne, please come . . . please come g-get me." She was crying and Wayne felt a strange tightness in his chest. "Please . . . I love you . . . please . . ."

He frowned and glanced at his dad, who was standing in the archway separating kitchen and hallway. The old man's eyes were bleary, his brow creased with concern.

Wayne shrugged and turned away. "Melissa, what's going on? Are you—"

"I'm s-still in this f-fucking place." More tears now. More sniffles. Then she composed herself and said, "I shouldn't be doing this. I managed to sneak out to the hall phone after lights out. Wayne, this place is horrible, worse than you can imagine. Please come get me out of here."

"What? How am I—"

Then she sucked in a startled breath. "Oh no. I've got to go. Someone's coming."

Wayne opened his mouth to ask more questions, but the line abruptly went dead.

His assuaged his dad's concerns with a made-up story and went back to bed. But the little sleep he got was fitful. He spent most of the long night staring at the dark ceiling and scheming. Then the next morning he talked his best friend into helping him break Melissa out of the SIMRC.

Steve knocked back a huge swallow of Southern Comfort, then spluttered as he nearly choked on the warm whiskey. He wiped his mouth with the back of a hand and offered the bottle to Wayne.

Wayne accepted the bottle and parked at the road's shoulder. He tipped whiskey into his mouth as he stared at the big white sign. He relished the sting of it on his tongue.

He sighed and passed the bottle back to Steve.

Then he finally answered his friend's question.

"I don't know how we're gonna do it, man. Not yet. But I'll tell you this. We're not leaving this place without Melissa, one way or another."

Two
Submission

The headmistress's office was large and well-appointed. The several pieces of furniture were all sturdy and expensive. The floor was hardwood varnished to a high gloss. The walls were adorned with several pieces of original art, all of which had been purchased for extravagant sums via telephone auction. A brick fireplace dominated one wall. A fire burned in it now. A large bearskin rug was stretched across the floor in front of the fireplace. Several sets of dark wood bookcases held numerous leather-bound volumes.

Anna thought it looked the kind of office a big oil tycoon or someone like that would have. Some fat high roller who liked to show off his wealth. The kind of man who always had a cigar in his mouth and ate steak for dinner every night. Then shat fat rolls of money every time he took a dump.

Not at all like the kind of office one would expect of the headmistress of a place like the SIMRC, an institution that traded in self-righteousness and so-called conservative values.

But Anna was used to such hypocrisy by now.

She sat in an uncomfortable chair opposite the headmistress's big oak desk. The chair was a tiny, rickety thing that wobbled and creaked every time she squirmed or fidgeted. The chair wobbled and creaked a lot. It was the one bit of furniture that didn't look like something Robin Leach would gush over on *Lifestyles of the Rich and Famous*. It wasn't part of the usual decor. The sole reason for its presence here tonight was to make Anna writhe in discomfort. The ridiculous outfit she was wearing added to her discomfort. Black stockings, high heels, a pleated short skirt meant to resemble those

9

worn by Catholic school girls, and a white blouse stiff with starch, which was at least one size too small.

This wasn't the normal attire of female students at the SIMRC. Those prim, conservative garments had been folded and were sitting in a neat stack in a leather recliner to her right. This was her "special" outfit, the one she wore every time she was brought to Miss Huffington's office for a late night "counseling session."

The headmistress was pretending to ignore her for the moment. Her attention was focused on an open file on the desk. The fortyish woman nodded occasionally as she read, pausing now and then to make a notation in the file. Sybil Huffington looked good for her age. She was tall and slender. Her hair was pinned back, but several long blonde strands hung loose and framed her cheeks in a way that made her somewhat plain face seem prettier, almost girlish.

Anna thought, *It could be worse.*

The bitch could be a warty old hag covered in liver spots.

Outside, thunder boomed. A flash of lightning lit up the big window behind the headmistress. The lights in the office flickered for a moment, but stayed on. Another crash of thunder followed quick on the heels of the last, this one so loud and violent it made Anna flinch.

She shifted her aching butt and the chair's legs groaned again. She hated the damn thing, but knew she wouldn't be in the uncomfortable little chair much longer. Miss Huffington enjoyed these torturous little mind games. She was a sadistic bitch. But there were other things she enjoyed more. Intimate things. She was torturing herself by stretching out the wait every bit as much as she was torturing Anna. Anna knew from experience the woman wouldn't be able to stand the exquisite anticipation much longer. She sure hoped so anyway. She wanted to get on with the evening's naughty escapades and then get back to her private room.

Most of the time she didn't much mind being Miss Huffington's little slave. There were benefits, after all. She had a room of her own, no fucking roommate to put up with, and she didn't have to put up with half the shit the other kids did. They were going to leave this place fundamentally changed. Forever. No more partying. No more sex. No more booze or drugs. No more rock and roll. The graduating boys would all go on to become soulless middle management automatons, or maybe republican party operatives, while the girls would all prepare for a future as good little Stepford wives in suburbia.

But not Anna.

In another few months she'd emerge from this place essentially the same person she'd been upon entering. She'd been spared the worst of the deprogramming training and was only required to go through the motions with the rest of it, just enough to keep up appearances. The price she paid was mostly loss of dignity and self-respect. But she would get over that.

Eventually.

Maybe.

Anna frowned.

She didn't like to dwell too deeply on the long-term implications of this situation. Hell, she didn't like to think about the future at all. It was this gray, nebulous thing lurking somewhere beyond the visible horizon. She had long subscribed to the live fast, die young, leave a pretty corpse aesthetic. And she'd always figured her end would be like Nancy Spungen's. Dead in some squalid hotel room in New York City or Paris. A needle in her arm or a knife in her gut. This didn't bother her. She looked forward to living as hard as possible prior to her rendezvous with dark fate.

Or maybe . . . just maybe . . . she'd grow out of all that.

Either way, it would be her choice. She would always remain captain of her own soul.

There were just a few hard things to get through first.

Miss Huffington snapped the file shut and looked at Anna with a smile. "It's time, dear."

Anna forced a smile of her own. "Yes, m'am."

11

She stood up and walked around to the other side of the desk. Miss Huffington pushed her chair back and stood, giving Anna room. Then Anna bent over and braced her hands against the edge of the desk. Miss Huffington moved into position behind her. She didn't do anything at first. More of this waiting bullshit. Anna looked at the bearskin rug. If things went the usual way, that's where the evening's festivities would conclude. At least the rug felt nice on her bare skin.

Another long, pregnant moment elapsed.

Anna heard Miss Huffington's breathing deepen.

Another burst of thunder shook the window behind them.

Then, finally, Miss Huffington lifted the hem of Anna's pleated skirt and pushed it up over her waist. Anna lifted her ass a bit higher. Then she felt the headmistress's hand on her bare buttocks. It rested there a moment. A light, almost gentle touch. A mockery of what was to come. Anna held her breath and swallowed hard.

Miss Huffington's hand came away from her ass.

Anna tensed.

Then she heard the headmistress's hand swooping through the air.

The blow landed. Hard. Anna rocked forward and gripped the edge of the desk more tightly.

You've been a very bad girl, Anna."

Anna gritted her teeth. "Yes, m'am."

"Do you regret your transgressions, dear?"

"Yes, m'am."

"I'm not sure I believe you, Anna. You've been naughty and require discipline."

Anna rolled her eyes.

Of course I do.

Miss Huffington's open palm struck her rear end again. Then again and again, over and over until Anna lost count of how many times she'd been struck. This was how it usually went. Soon Miss Huffington would pause briefly between blows to lightly caress her exposed buttocks. Then there would be more blows. And, eventually,

Anna would feel the tentative probe of a finger. And soon after that any pretense of discipline would end and they would move this party over to the bearskin rug.

But Anna was wrong.

Miss Huffington did deviate from the routine she'd established with the young girl.

And for Anna, nothing would ever be the same again.

Three
Garbageman

Digging a grave was always nasty work. Dirty and time-consuming work. Everett Quigley wasn't a gravedigger by profession, but in his time as chief maintenance man at the SIMRC he'd been called upon to dig three of the things. And now a fourth. He hadn't exactly enjoyed it the first three times, but at least on those occasions the weather had been nice. Although the work had been exhausting, he'd been able to take his time with it, had even been able to take frequent breaks. Unfortunately, a leisurely pace wasn't possible tonight.

Leave it to Miss Huffingtwat to kill a bitch in the middle of a goddamned thunderstorm.

With a grunt he thrust the shovel blade into the wet earth, scooped up another load of mud, and tossed it onto the growing pile beside the big hole. The hole was maybe three feet deep at this point, about half what it needed to be, and at this rate he'd be out here another hour before he was done. The job had to be done right. You couldn't half-ass a thing like this. The hole had to be deep enough to prevent animals from digging the dead bitch up.

He paused in his work to glance at the sky. The rain was still coming down in thick sheets. The thunder and lightning hadn't let up either. Everett cursed the headmistress again and prayed he could get this over with before one of those silver-white electric daggers struck him and turned him into two-hundred pounds of human hamburger. It was insane that he was being made to do this tonight. He'd begged Huffington to let him stash the corpse somewhere safe until the storm had passed, but she'd insisted that the job be done immediately. And so he was doing it. He'd had no real choice. Everett was an ex-con with a record longer than the average Stephen King novel. After being paroled this latest time, he'd had little luck finding gainful employment with any kind of legit business. Until, that is, he'd finally caught a break and got hired on by the SIMRC.

Well, he'd *thought* he was catching a break.

Way it turned out, Sybil Huffington had been looking for a man with his kind of dubious background. A man she could trust to perform certain kinds of sensitive errands. Corpse disposal, of course, but also the procurement of illegal drugs and "outside entertainment." The latter was a typical Huffington euphemism. In this case it referred to strung-out hookers willing to do anything for a buck. He'd buried two of the skinny whores out here in the woods that bordered the SIMRC property. The girl tonight was only the second SIMRC enrollee she'd offed. And Everett hoped she'd be the last for a while. The girl's sudden disappearance from the center would cause questions. The cops would come sniffing around, same as last time. And Miss Huffington would tell them the girl had chafed under the center's strict behavior policies and had simply run away. A believable enough story. The kid had been a delinquent. They all were. Running away was the kind of thing a kid like that would do. Hell, it was what Everett would do in their place. Even so, the cops weren't stupid. They'd take a closer look at things out here if the kids started "running away" too frequently.

And then things would get mighty uncomfortable in a hurry.

Everett put the matter out of his head. It was a thing to worry about later, if at all. Maybe after he was back in his apartment. After a long, hot shower and a calming glass or two of bourbon. Then he could devote some time to thinking of ways to extricate himself from this fucked-up situation. Or maybe not. Maybe he would just get drunk and try not to think about all the bad things he'd done over the last couple of years. Like always.

He slammed the shovel blade into the ground yet again, grimacing as it scraped stone. He yanked the blade out of the wet earth and tried again in another spot. Another scrape of stone on metal. Three more shovel probes yielded the same result.

15

"Fuck!"

The water at the bottom of the hole was up around his ankles and rising. The hell with it. Four feet down would have to be good enough. He tossed the shovel out of the hole and started to climb out. The soil at the edge of the hole was loose and mushy beneath his gloved fingers. He almost slid back into the hole, but at last managed to haul himself out.

The girl's body was wrapped in a tarp at the edge of the small clearing. He trudged over to it and grabbed an end of the rolled-up dead girl. Huffing and grunting, he dragged her over to the grave. The muscles in his arms and shoulders tensed as he readied himself to heave the body into the hole. But he hesitated. A strange and powerful impulse to have a look at the girl before he consigned her to the earth gripped him. It puzzled him. It was morbid and not like him at all. He wasn't some sicko. Hell no. He was simply a regular guy who'd made a lot of dumb choices in his life and was stuck in a bad situation. But the urge to check the body out was strong and undeniable.

He set the tarp down and reached inside his yellow rain slicker to extract an X-Acto knife from his tool belt. Then he knelt and used the knife to slice through the thick layers of duct tape he had used to seal the girl up in the tarp. In another few moments he was rolling the tarp open, and then there she was.

His breath caught in his throat.

And he felt a swelling against the crotch of his jeans. A flush of deep shame followed, but the excitement remained.

This isn't me, insisted a desperate, clamoring voice from the depths of his mind. *I'm not a bad guy. I'm not like this.*

The rain quickly soaked the dead girl's hair and the absurd school girl outfit. Her wet, glistening face looked more delicate now, almost angelic. Beautiful. He placed a hand on one of the girl's pale thighs and shuddered at the sweet softness. He grunted. His nostrils flared. His cock pushed and strained against the fabric of his jeans. His moved his trembling hand along a cold inner thigh, his fingers

16

brushing over an intricate tattoo of some shirtless and scrawny rock star leaning over a microphone. The tattoo included two words at the bottom: RAW POWER. Then his fingers moved past the tattoo and slid beneath the hem of the pleated skirt. In another moment his fingers were entering her. He started working at the clasps of his rain slicker with his free hand.

Then white light filled the sky.

Everett's head snapped up. He frowned at the white streak moving quicksilver fast across the sky. At first he thought it must be an especially spectacular blast of lightning, but he dismissed this idea an instant later. The white streak trailed what looked like a blazing ball of fire. The object was coming in low and fast, and looked to be burning brighter the nearer it got to the ground.

Everett gulped. "A fuckin' meteor. Shit."

Terror flashed through him as he tracked the meteor's trajectory and realized it would likely hit somewhere in the vicinity of the clearing. Everett yanked his fingers out of the dead girl's pussy and stood bolt upright. His head was still turned toward the sky. His jaw hung slack as he watched the great, fiery orb bearing down on him. He felt like a doomed man standing on train tracks and watching the approach of the Hellbound Express. His legs shook. He whimpered.

The meteor was coming down too fast.

There was nowhere to go.

Except . . .

He glanced down and loosed a burst of mad, helpless laughter.

The light above burned brighter than ever, enveloping the clearing in a warm glow like daylight. A roaring filled his ears and his mind screamed at him to jump.

He jumped.

Another moment passed. The air above crackled and hissed.

The ground began to shake.

Then the explosion came, a sound so huge and all-encompassing that for a time it seemed to obliterate all of existence.

Four
Light Up the Sky

The convenience store was two miles down the road from the Southern Illinois Music Re-Education Center. Wayne turned into the Kwik Mart's parking lot and parked next to a phone booth. Another crack of lightning lit up the sky as he pawed through the pockets of his leather jacket for change. The search produced thirty cents in dimes and nickels, more than enough.

"So I'm gonna call my dad, let him know we've arrived safely at your mom's place."

Steve Wade snorted. "Right. Dear ol' mom." He grinned, but there was a disturbing emptiness in his eyes. "Can't wait to see the bitch."

Steve almost never talked about his mother. Carol Wade had deserted her family several years earlier. Wayne rarely questioned his friend about it. It was clear he was still haunted by it, so Wayne had been shocked when Steve suggested a trip to see his mother as a cover story for their highly illicit expedition.

Wayne arched a brow. "Does she really live around here?"

Steve shrugged. "She did as of a couple years ago, anyway." He grunted. "Like to drop in on her and give her a piece of my mind. Stupid whore."

Wayne frowned. "Huh."

An awkward silence followed. Then Wayne blew out a breath and reached for the door handle, pausing a moment to steel himself for the ordeal ahead. The phone booth was less than a dozen feet from the driver's side door, but the distance may as well have been the length of a football field.

Then he thought, *Fuck it. Stop being such a pussy.*

He pulled the handle and shoved the door open. A gust of wind lashed rain sideways into the Jeep. He leaped out and threw the door shut behind him as he dashed toward the phone booth. He jumped over the curb, splashed through a puddle, and hurled himself through the open door. He slammed the door shut and shook like a wet dog. Water streamed off of him and pattered on the phone booth floor.

He shivered and picked up the phone's receiver, cradled it between ear and shoulder, and dropped the dimes into the coin slot. He got a dial tone and heaved a sigh of relief. The phone's dial was one of the old rotary jobs. A real relic. He hooked a finger in one of the little holes and began to spin the dial. As he dialed the last number, he became aware of a bright light filling the booth. He glanced up as the first ring sounded in his ear, frowning at a bright white streak coming in low over the horizon.

"What the fuck?"

The line clicked and his dad answered the phone. "Devereaux residence."

The white streak flashed by overhead and Wayne turned to watch it head in the general direction of the SIMRC. "Holy shit."

"Wayne?"

Only then did he realize his dad had answered. "Uh . . . hi, dad."

"Son, are you okay?" His father's voice was tinged with mild concern. But Wayne knew Tom Devereaux trusted his only son to act responsibly. It would never occur to the man to think his son might be up to something truly reckless. A stab of guilt made him frown. "Are you and Steve at his mom's house?"

"Uh . . . yeah. Got here about a half hour ago."

"Uh huh." A pause. There was something in his father's tone that made his stomach clench. Maybe the old man wasn't as blindly trusting as Wayne thought. "Look, Wayne, can I talk to Steve's mom for a second?"

Oh, shit.

Wayne's stomach did a slow roll. A moment of blind panic almost tripped him up. Then he thought of Melissa and snapped out of it. In that moment a plausible-sounding excuse popped into his head, and he smiled. "Afraid not, dad. Carol isn't feeling well and went to bed early. She stayed up just long enough to see Steve."

"Uh huh." Tom Devereaux sighed. "Well, you boys stay out of trouble. See you Sunday, son."

"See ya, dad."

The line went dead and Wayne returned the receiver to the cradle. He muscled the booth's door open and trudged back to the Jeep, not hurrying because there wasn't much of a point—he couldn't get a whole lot fucking wetter than he already was. Soon he was back inside the Jeep and again ensconced behind the steering wheel.

Steve was wired like a motherfucker. Like a dude who'd just done a whole 8-ball of coke all by himself. He bounced in his seat, barely able to contain the wild energy thrumming within him. "Dude! Did you not fucking see that fucking comet or whatever it was? That was *amazing*! I've never seen any shit like that in my whole fucking life, dude! I mean, shit, did you *see* that?"

"I saw it."

Steve cackled. "Well . . . was that fucking amazing, or was that not fucking amazing?"

"It was pretty impressive."

"Fuck yeah, it was."

"I also saw that it was headed in the general direction of the center."

"Oh." Steve instantly sobered. He glanced over his shoulder at the Jeep's rear window. "Yeah. You're right. Shit." He looked at Wayne. "Um . . . I'm sure it didn't hit the center, man. Melissa . . . she'll be all right."

"I don't think it hit the center. The meteor, or whatever it was, was coming in too low to make it all the way out there. Might've hit somewhere in the vicinity, though."

"Right, right. That's what I think, too. No doubt about it, man."

Steve's tone belied his words, though. He wasn't sure. Wayne wasn't either, really. But it was pointless to freak out over it. He was no superhero. He couldn't leap into the sky and swat the thing back into space. It was going to do whatever it was going to do. Period. End of story.

Regardless, he did feel a greater sense of urgency now. He twisted around in his seat and reached through the gap between the seats to snag a burlap sack nestled in the floor behind the passenger seat. He'd swiped the sack from the utility shed back home. It was old and grimy. Stenciled on the side in black block letters were the words US ARMY.

Steve was frowning as Wayne settled in behind the steering wheel again. "What's in the stinky old bag, dude?"

"I'll show you. Don't freak out."

Steve snorted. "Right. Like I'd do that." His frown returned. "Unless you've got some dude's head in there. You don't…do you?"

Wayne uncinched the sack's drawstring and pulled it open. Then he reached inside and withdrew its contents.

Steve's eyes bugged out like those of a cartoon character. His mouth dropped open. "Whoa."

In Wayne's hands were a Colt .45 automatic and a Walther 9mm. The guns belonged to his dad, who had inherited them from his father. They were old and hadn't been oiled or used in a lot of years. His dad had stashed them on a high shelf in the utility shed long ago and had probably forgotten he even owned them. There'd been a fair amount of rust on each weapon, but Wayne had done his best to sand away the most obvious brown patches. They looked almost like new now.

Steve shook his head. "Dude. No. You can't be serious."

"What do you mean?"

"What're we doing here, blasting our way in and out like a couple of old time outlaws?"

21

Wayne smirked. "What, you think I'm crazy?" He passed the Walther to Steve. "They're not loaded. And I don't have any ammunition for them. They're for intimidation purposes only, to be used only as a last resort. If we find ourselves in a situation where we have to get past a security guard or some other asshole, we haul these out and wave them around, acting all hardass and shit."

Steve grinned. "Psychological motherfuckin' warfare."

Wayne nodded. "Something like that. The sight of the guns alone will be enough to make most people think twice about fucking with us."

"They'll be too busy shittin' their pants to get in our way. Fuck it. Let's do this. But it's my turn to pick the tunes."

"Okay."

Wayne put the Jeep in gear as Steve opened the glove compartment and began to root through the assortment of cassette tapes stored there. Steve's taste ran toward the heavier stuff. Slayer, Metallica, Diamond Head, Mercyful Fate, like that. Patches for many of these bands were sewn into the fabric of his denim jacket. He found something apparently suitable, snapped open the case, and slapped the tape into the cassette player. He cranked the volume knob to the right as Wayne guided the Jeep back onto the road and stomped on the accelerator.

The roar of the music rattled the Jeep's interior.

The Misfits. *Horror Business.*

A surprising choice, given Steve's tastes. Wayne grinned his approval and sang along at the top of his lungs as the Jeep rocketed toward the SIMRC and back into the thick of the storm.

Five
Children of the Grave

The ringing in his ears had only just begun to fade by the time Everett realized he was still alive. The blazing wrecking ball masquerading as a meteor hadn't pulverized him after all. So he was lucky in the most important way. Still had a pulse. Downside, he was lying at the bottom of a dead girl's grave, covered in filth and muck and choking on several inches of standing rainwater.

He forced himself to his knees and sat there for several long moments. He still needed some time to gather his strength, but at least now he wouldn't drown. He shivered and his teeth chattered. The temperature was around forty degrees. Not arctic conditions, but more than cold enough to render an already unpleasant situation downright miserable. At last he could stand it no longer and climbed out of the grave. He saw immediately how close a call he'd had and shuddered. The meteor had skimmed over the clearing, then had crashed through a line of trees, tracing a blackened path deeper into the woods. He could see the smoking crater from where he sat. The meteor itself lay in several smoking, glowing pieces. It was smaller than he'd imagined. Big enough to obliterate anything in its path, of course, but intact it'd been maybe the size of a van. On approach, of course, it'd seemed about as big as the sun.

The reality of his survival and its implications began to sink in. He didn't think anyone who'd noticed the meteor's descent would come out to investigate on a night as nasty as this one. But it wouldn't be smart to base any decisions on that assumption. There was still a dead girl to put in the ground. He'd best get it done and get the fuck gone before any looky-loos came poking around. And no more messing with the dead babe's goodies either. He remembered those strange moments before the approach of the meteor and experienced a moment of profound self-revulsion. He figured maybe being around Miss Huffington had scrambled his brain some. Some of her depravity had rubbed off on him. And it didn't take a genius to figure things would only get worse if he continued to stick around and do her dirty work.

"That's it, I'm leavin' this fuckin' place."

A coughing fit overtook him and he glanced again in the direction of the crater. The pieces were still glowing. Some kind of weird bright green color. And shit, they were emitting something toxic, too. A white mist swirled over the blackened landscape and drifted into the clearing. Another coughing fit came over him as the fumes invaded his nostrils and made his eyes water. He began to panic. No telling what fucked-up kind of outer space gunk that thing had been carrying. It could be poisoning him even now.

He fished a rag from a rear pocket of his jeans and held the wet bit of cloth over his face. Then he reached for the dead girl. Enough was enough. Get the bitch in the ground. That's what he had to do. Right now. He seized her by a wrist and got up on his haunches. He gave her a tug and she rolled onto her side. Then a very surprising thing happened.

To understate on an epic level.

The dead girl twisted out of his grip and seized him by the wrist. This was so far beyond the scope of anything Everett would have considered possible that he could only gape and watch in numb disbelief as she pulled his hand toward her face. He only snapped out of it when she drew his fingers into her mouth. By then it was too late.

Everett tried to yank his hand away, but her grip was surprisingly strong. She held him fast and bit down on his fingers. He screamed as teeth penetrated flesh and began to grind away at bone. She thrashed her head violently, like a dog with a piece of raw meat. At that point Everett was doing some thrashing of his own. Desperation triggered an adrenaline burst that hit his veins like lightning. He managed to get free of her and fell backward onto his ass. He held his mangled hand up and saw bright arterial blood spurting from the place where three of his fingers had been. The pain was immense. He covered the wound with the cloth he'd used to keep out the fumes, clamping down hard. That ratcheted the pain up many more notches, introduced him to a level of soul-shearing agony he wouldn't have imagined possible prior to this night.

He looked at the not-dead girl. She looked like a wild animal chewing on his severed fingers. Her eyes were dull and glassy, like those of a wax figure. On some level, Everett realized that although her physical body had reanimated, her mind was still gone. This wasn't a human being that had attacked him. Not really. It was a thing. A monster.

It was a . . . oh hell, it was a fucking zombie.

And if there was one thing Everett knew about zombies, it was that they never stopped being hungry.

If you believed all the movies, that is.

And right now, Everett fucking believed them.

Dawn of the Dead?

A goddamn documentary.

The zombie girl stopped chewing and a large lump—his masticated fingers—slid slowly down her gullet. The sight of it sent a fresh wave of revulsion through Everett. It occurred to him those were the very fingers with which he'd probed her pussy. There was a kind of poetic justice at work there, if you could look at it objectively.

Everett began to realize how light-headed he was feeling. Whether it was from blood loss, the toxic fumes he'd inhaled, or a combination of both, he didn't know. And didn't care. He had to get out of these goddamned woods. Pronto.

Then the zombie's head turned toward him and its dull eyes fixed on him. The creature got to its feet and began to move stiffly toward him, hands reaching for him as it groaned and drooled. Instinct caused Everett to scoot backward, an act that caused him to slam his injured hand against the ground. He howled in agony and flopped onto his side. But that old survival instinct wouldn't allow him to surrender to the inevitable just yet. He rolled onto his stomach and used his good hand to push himself to his knees. The zombie wasn't moving too fast. He could outrun it if he could just get up.

This was what he was thinking as another improbable thing occurred nearby. A section of earth three or four feet to his left began to shift. He recognized the patch of ground as being a place where he'd dug a grave for one of the skinny whores. His mouth dropped open as he watched a scrawny hand punch through the wet earth.

He groaned. "Oh, fuck me. This isn't happening."

But it was.

The prostitute clawed her way out of the grave with stunning swiftness. Though somewhat decayed and covered in muck, she was still recognizable. She'd called herself Candy Caine. Caine as in cocaine. Street name, of course. Sybil Huffington had choked the life out of her only a month ago. He recognized the tight black vinyl hot pants and tube top he'd buried her in. Though much of her flesh remained, some burrowing, underground thing had chewed her eyes out. She nonetheless was able to get a fix on him as she came the rest of the way out of her grave. She opened her mouth and spit out dirt as she staggered toward him. He noticed with dread that her teeth looked to be in fine shape. Just his luck. The only streetwalker in all the world with perfect movie star choppers happened to be the one bent on devouring him.

Distracted by the awful specter of Candy's improbable resurrection, he'd momentarily forgotten all about the threat approaching from the rear.

Anna Kincaid seized his arm and clamped her mouth over the meaty part above the elbow. He screamed again and tried to tear free. His flesh stretched like taffy, muscle and sinew tearing as a fresh eruption of bright red blood spattered Anna's face. Then she wrenched her head and tore loose a big chunk of Everett meat. He screamed yet again and fell away from her as she worked on this tasty new morsel.

Candy pounced on him then, and he screamed one last time.

The scent of decaying flesh filled his nostrils as Candy's questing mouth found his throat and savagely ripped it out. The zombies savaged the rest of his body while he was still warm. While they worked on him, two more zombies—both quite a bit riper than Candy—clawed their way out of their graves. In a while the dead girls, guided by some instinct they wouldn't have been able to understand even if they'd been able to think about it, staggered out of the clearing as a loose group.

Toward the SIMRC.

Before long, what remained of Everett got up and followed them.

Six
Video Nasty

Though she maintained a separate residence in a nearby affluent neighborhood, Sybil Huffington spent the bulk of her leisure time in the lavish apartment adjacent to her SIMRC office. The house was just for the sake of appearances. She held a position of respect in the community. Certain things were expected of one in her position. The house, of course. Also, a woman of her stature within the conservative Christian community was expected to have a husband, preferably a wealthy one.

Sybil Huffington did not want a husband.

Or even a boyfriend.

She'd endured one sham of a marriage for ten years. Never again, she had sworn. However, by the time she was finally able to be honest with herself about her true preferences, she'd become too invested in the world of Christian activism to start over again from scratch as a . . . what, a gay activist?

Absurd. Impossible.

She was stuck.

She'd accepted this years ago. But one of Sybil's strengths had always been her problem-solving skills. She simply needed an outlet, a discreet means of indulging her true desires while maintaining her public persona as a paragon of conservatism. Hence her recruitment of the ex-convict. Her carnal encounters with the whores he'd found had thrilled her in the beginning. The thrill was twofold, a long sought after physical release, as well as a weird psychological kick derived from being intimate with women so far below her station in life. Bottom line, she was slumming. She was their better in every way.

28

Richer, prettier, and smarter than all of them put together. And yet she'd been the one paying them to provide physical pleasure. What was truly amazing was how there was virtually no limit to what the whores would let her do to them as long as she paid them enough. She found she liked being rough with them, even abusive.

Liked it a bit too much, as it turned out.

The first death rattled her, was nearly her undoing. She had even considered calling 911. But the prospect of the sure-to-ensue scandal trumped any notions of doing the "morally right" thing. So she'd summoned Quigley. An arrangement was made. The ex-con received a very nice bonus in his next paycheck. Weeks passed. Then months. After a while she began to realize she would get away with the whore's murder. There would never be a price to pay.

Eventually the desire to experience those same thrills again became too much. Quigley delivered another whore, who she treated almost as roughly as the one she'd killed. The experience emboldened her, left her craving a new level of thrill. Thus began the tentative process of identifying who among the female population at the SIMRC might be open to certain possibilities. It didn't take long. Delinquents were not hard to bribe. Of course, there was a greater level of risk involved. The parents of these children were paying good money to have their offspring restored to a morally righteous path. Any allegations of impropriety would bring her world crashing down. But Sybil did it anyway. And she treated the SIMRC girls as roughly as she'd treated the whores. It was crazy. She knew that. But the higher risk level only made it more exciting. She sometimes wondered whether some secret part of her hoped something would go wrong. Certainly she was pushing the envelope harder than ever, with two SIMRC girls dead by her hands.

Speaking of which . . .

Sybil turned on the television in her living room and popped the videotape into the VCR. The tape was new and bore a label with the handwritten words GIRL 4. Her not-so-subtle code for fourth dead girl. She of course taped all her sessions with both the whores and the SIMRC girls. The actual physical experiences were the best, but getting to relive them all endlessly via the modern marvel of videotape was almost as good.

She settled into a leather sofa and opened the front of her bathrobe. On the screen there was an initial moment of fuzzy static, but this quickly resolved itself into a shot of the desk in her office. The videotaped image showed her sitting behind the desk as she pretended to read a file. Sybil picked up the remote and fast-forwarded through several moments of this tedium, then pushed play at the point when Anna Kincaid stood up and walked around the desk. She set the remote down and slid a hand between her legs, felt the moistness that was already there. Her breath grew short as she watched herself stand and left the hem of Anna's dress.

Then the phone rang.

"Shit!"

The phone sat on an end table to her left. She glared at the device as it rang again. And then again. One more full ring and her answering machine would pick up. She wanted to let that happen. But if the person calling was who she suspected . . .

She snatched the receiver up and barked at the caller: "What!"

Masculine laughter, unperturbed and casual. Insidious. The sound of it made Sybil want to vomit. "Sybil, darling, have I caught you at a bad time?"

She suppressed a groan.

It was Mark Cheney, one of the instructors in her employ.

"I'm busy, Mark. What do you want?"

He chuckled. "Oh, I think you know."

Fuck.

This man was the bane of her existence. One day a month or so back he'd walked into her office late in the work day and caught her in the company of one of the hookers. Nothing had been happening. The woman was just there, seated in a chair opposite the big oak desk. But the whore's mere presence in her office had been proof enough of impropriety.

She'd been impatient and hornier than usual that day. Utilizing a degree of stealth worthy of a special forces commander, Quigley had managed to smuggle the woman in ahead of the technical end of the work day. However, in her haste to get laid, she'd neglected to lock the outer door to her office. Cheney had been out of line for walking into her office unannounced, but she blamed only herself for what had happened. The door should have been locked, end of story.

So far, she'd been lucky. Cheney hadn't told anyone of the incident. And he had vowed to stay mum on the subject—for a price

And he was a greedy bastard.

He'd gotten a raise and his hours had been cut.

He had the use of a company car, and, when he felt like it, the use of Sybil Huffington's body.

Sybil sighed. "I'm tired, Mark. It's been a long day."

Cheney made a tsk-tsk noise. "And it's about to get a little longer. I want to do the usual things with you, Sybil. Believe it or not, though, I'll also have an actual work-related matter to discuss with you."

Sybil frowned. "Oh?"

"It's about one of the students, a Melissa Campbell."

Sybil's brow creased as her mind worked to place the name with a face. And soon she had it. Melissa Campbell was a cute little blonde from some nowhere town, sent to the SIMRC for all the usual reasons. Sybil could recall nothing at all unusual from the girl's file.

"What about her?"

"Ah . . . well . . ."

It wasn't like Mark to hem and haw. He liked to get to the point. Something was bothering him. Sybil pushed the pause button on the remote and set it aside. "Spit it out, man."

Cheney cleared his throat and said, "Well . . . as you may know, the girl is one of my students. The other day she misbehaved during my lecture and I ordered her to my office. And . . . well . . ." He sighed again. He really didn't want to say whatever it was. Sybil began to smile, relishing her tormentor's discomfort. "The thing is, I may have been a tad too harsh in dispensing discipline this time."

Sybil's smile broadened to a grin. The parents of SIMRC students were all required to sign a waiver authorizing the use of corporal punishment. Paddlings, often quite severe, were commonplace. For Mark to be worried, something truly awful must have happened.

"You better tell me all about it."

That broke the dam. Cheney's account of the encounter with Melissa Campbell spilled forth in a rush. And it was every bit as dreadful as she'd hoped. Not as genuinely depraved as her own escapades, but shocking nonetheless. By any normal standards, it would mean the end of his career in the re-education business. It could even mean a stint in jail, should word of it ever get out.

"So that's why I need to see you tonight. You have to help me figure out what to do."

Sybil's eyes glittered with malice. Mark would have shuddered at the sight of it. "Of course, dear. I'll call down to the guard house, let them know you're coming."

"Thank you, Sybil. Oh, and, ah . . ." He laughed again, and that smooth, oily confidence he'd exuded before was back. "Don't be wearing any clothes when I get there. I want to do some things to you before we discuss that awful child."

Sybil's grin froze in place. She forced a laugh. "Of course, dear."

She returned the phone to its cradle and picked up the remote again, fast-forwarded to the part where she was sitting atop Anna Kincaid on the bearskin rug. They were both nude, their bodies glistening with sweat. Mark was maybe fifteen minutes away. Sybil knew she would require some stimulation before his arrival, otherwise she wouldn't be able to perform with him.

She pushed the play button.

And watched herself strangle the life out of a human being.

Then she rewound the tape and watched it again.

Seven
Jailbreak

Melissa Campbell waited until she was sure her roommate was asleep. Then she threw aside the blanket covering her still fully-clothed body, reached under the bed to retrieve the bag she'd stashed there earlier, and cautiously began to make her way across the room. When she reached the door, she clicked a button on her digital watch. The LED display lit up and showed her the time: 9:59 pm.

Talk about cutting it close.

She waited another minute. At 10:00 she rapped softly three times on the door and held her breath. A long moment elapsed. The moment lengthened to a full minute. She put a hand over her mouth to muffle a whimper. Then she clicked the button again.

10:01.

She knew she shouldn't panic yet. They'd agreed on 10:00. They'd even synchronized their watches, like spies in some old war movie. But any number of things could be delaying him. She would give him a little more leeway, perhaps as long as fifteen minutes. After that, it would be clear that something unforeseen had occurred to derail their plans.

Yet another check of the watch.

10:02 became 10:03.

She pressed her ear to the door and strained to hear something, anything. But the hallway beyond the door remained tomb-silent. Melissa sagged against the door and fought hard to push back a burgeoning sob. She'd been so sure she was getting out of this horrible place tonight. She was scheduled to attend another of Mr. Cheney's lectures tomorrow, and the suddenly very real possibility of again being in his presence filled her with dread.

She'd been stupid to mouth off during one of his bogus speeches about the "corrosive effect" of heavy metal music on the spiritual lives of young people. Talking back just wasn't allowed at the SIMRC. But corporal punishment was allowed, and its implementation was a given in all instances of disobedience and insubordination. She'd expected a paddling in the wake of referring to Mr. Cheney and his fellow instructors at the SIMRC as "thought police".

She had not, however, been prepared for what actually did happen in Cheney's office. It had begun in the usual way, with a request that she bend over and brace her hands against the edge of his desk. Having no choice, she obeyed. He then took his time getting down to business, lecturing her about the necessity of finding her way back to the true and righteous path. Her soul was in peril, he told her. Satan had his claws in her already. If she failed to reject evil in all its guises—such as liberal philosophies in general, and the negative influence of heavy metal in particular—she would wind up in hell, where she would endure agonies beyond imagining for all eternity.

At some point he stopped laying the bullshit on her long enough to unlock a drawer in his desk, from which he removed a long, wooden paddle with several holes drilled in it. He then moved into position behind her and placed the paddle flat against her ass, leaving it there for a long moment.

"Is any of this registering with you, young lady?" he asked in a voice grown suddenly hoarse. "Are you ready to accept Jesus Christ as your lord and savior?"

And she just hadn't been able to help it, the words springing to her mouth too fast to call back. "Oh, just get on with it, Toad-man."

"Toad-man" was what many at SIMRC called Mr. Cheney in private conversation, and it was an apt description. He was short and thick through the middle, with doughy flesh below his chin and too-pink lips that made him look like . . . well, like a toad.

Seething, he spoke through gritted teeth: "What . . . did . . . you . . . say?"

In those moments, she'd felt like she was hanging from the edge of a high cliff by her fingertips. It was easier to just let go. She lashed out again. "You heard me, Toad-man." She looked over her shoulder then and saw how red his fat face had become. "I don't buy any of your bullshit. You're right, you know. Satan's got his big red claws in me, and I fucking love it. I can't wait to suck his giant red cock in hell."

Looking back, she couldn't believe the things she'd said. She should have known she was going too far. But she could not have known what was about to happen.

He drew the paddle back and swung it forward with all his might, swatting her hard enough to send her sprawling against the desk. Then he did it again. And again. Hitting her harder than anyone had ever hit her before. Over and over. It hurt. Oh fuck, had it hurt. She cried. Begged him to stop. But he kept hitting her. And he raged at her, calling her all sorts of names, the worst she'd ever heard. Like nothing else she'd ever heard from the mouth of a supposedly righteous man. Then she heard the clatter of the paddle hitting the floor. Next she felt his weight on top of her, pressing her against the desk, robbing her of her breath. The feel of his hard-on brought a rush of bile to her mouth. She begged him to stop, but he wouldn't. He lifted her dress and pushed her panties down. Dropped his trousers and forced his way in, raped her right there in his office, the son of a bitch, holding his meaty hand over her mouth to muffle her cries. She was a virgin. There was blood. It was all sweaty and messy, and it was the worst thing that had ever happened to her. The worst thing that could *ever* happen to her, and after it was over she wanted to die.

And he told her, "You must never speak of this to anyone. Not ever. If you do, I'll hire someone to kill you."

She believed him and made the promise he wanted to hear. Then she returned to her room and began to plot her escape. She couldn't bear the idea of staying here even one more day, much less through the end of the school year. That night she'd managed to place her tearful call to Wayne. The next day she'd realized this was a mistake. Wayne couldn't help her. He was just a kid, as powerless as she was. She would have to do this herself.

With maybe a little help.

She clicked the button on her watch again.

10:07.

She sighed.

And then she heard a very soft sound from the other side of the door, something that might have been the tread of feet on the tiled floor. A light, cautious sound. Then the sound stopped and she heard someone breathing. She curled her right hand into a fist to still the trembling.

Then she rapped softly on the door three times.

The signal they'd arranged.

She glanced down and saw the silver doorknob began to turn. There a small metallic snick and the door began to move inward, muted light from the hallway spilling into the room. Then she saw his face and tears of joy filled her eyes. She rushed through the opening and threw her arms around him, burying her wet face against his neck.

David Heinrich, a gay punk kid from Chicago, returned the embrace and whispered in her ear. "Hush, girl. We need to get moving."

She stepped out of the embrace and stared up at him, still smiling. "I know, I know. I'm sorry. I see you got the key."

David grinned and flashed a wedge of silver, the key he'd used to unlock her door. Then he closed a palm around it and said, "Mr. Closet Case got very distracted while I was blowing him in the broom closet this afternoon."

Mr. Closet Case was what David called Henry Wilkins, a day shift guard at the SIMRC.

Melissa slung the strap of her bag over a shoulder. "Lucky for us. Will that get us out the back way?"

David shrugged. "Don't know. Not sure we'll even need it after this." He put a hand on her shoulder, steering her away from the open door. "Enough yakking. Let's move."

Melissa nodded. She didn't need convincing on that part. She turned to reach for the doorknob when a lamp inside the room suddenly snapped on.

"Hey!" the voice of Lindy Wallace, her roommate, cried out. "Melissa, what's going on?"

Melissa groaned, her dreams of escape dying abruptly in that moment.

Lindy's voice was so loud. Someone would hear. Someone would come.

Lindy was sitting up in bed, her arm extended toward the lamp behind her. Her eyes were bleary and she was dressed in her pajamas. She hopped out of the bed and padded over to them. Melissa remained rooted to the spot as the girl approached, helpless to do anything else, paralyzed by panic. Lindy stuck her head through the open doorway, gawked for a moment at David, who glared at her, and then turned a disbelieving gaze on Melissa.

"Holy shit. Are you guys escaping?"

Melissa heaved a sigh. No point denying it now. "We were, at least until you opened your big mouth."

She glanced up and down the hallway. Still empty. But someone was bound to show up soon.

Then Lindy surprised her. "Let me come with you."

Melissa blinked. "Um . . ."

"Fuck." David invested the one word with enough scorn to make both girls flinch. He turned Melissa around and pushed her back into the room. He pushed the door most of the way shut, holding it open with a finger. Then he directed a sneer at Lindy. "Throw some clothes on, girl."

"Yay!" Lindy bounced up and down like an idiot.

Melissa wanted to slap her.

But the girl surprised her again, quickly doing as she was told. She rooted through the drawers of a dresser and was fully clothed in just over a minute.

David opened the door again and peered around its edge to check that the way was still clear.

It was.

And they filed out of the room, David shutting the door behind them. They hurried down the empty hallway, clattered down the staircase, and within moments had made it to the bottom floor of the building. Melissa was stunned by how smoothly their exodus from the building had been to this point.

Then they reached a rear door, where they paused long enough for David to peer through a frosted glass window.

He frowned. "Huh. That's weird."

Melissa pushed him aside and peered through the same window. Her mouth dropped open. It took her a moment to process what she was seeing, and even then she could make no sense of it.

She looked at David. "What the fuck is up with that?"

David shook his head. "I don't know. They look . . . all fucked up."

Eight
Something in the Way

The rain had slackened some by the time the SIMRC building came into view. The flashes of lightning and booms of thunder became less frequent. But the journey back to the center had been slowed by a bit of rotten luck. A late model Cadillac had slipped into position in front of them from a side road early on and had remained there the whole way back, maintaining a steady pace of about fifteen miles beneath the speed limit as the two vehicles crawled along the snaking rural road. Wayne fumed and hurled curses at the Cad's driver. Because while it made sense to exercise some degree of caution on a road as dark and windy as this one, especially in these conditions, this was taking caution to insane extremes. The weather was improving. There were no other vehicles on the road.

It was maddening.

Though he had been tempted to pass the Cad, Wayne had elected to play it safe instead of letting his frustration get the better of him. It was still very wet out there. He didn't want to go slewing into a ditch when Melissa was counting on him. So when the two vehicles went around a bend and the SIMRC building loomed into view, he breathed a sigh of relief. "Finally."

Steve turned off the radio and lit the cigarette he'd just wedged into a corner of his mouth. "You know what your ride needs, bro? Side-mounted missiles. Some James Bond kinda shit like that."

Wayne grunted. "Yeah. No shit."

The Cadillac's left blinker came on, a steady red pulse in the darkness.

Steve flipped his Zippo shut and dropped it in a front pocket of his denim jacket. "Well, shit. Look where slowpoke is going."

Wayne laid a hand on the gearshift. His heart began to gallop. What he was about to do was both reckless and highly illegal. Doing this would be the true point of no return. He could go to jail for what he was about to do. Thinking about the hard reality of the situation terrified him.

Fuck it.

"Hold tight."

Steve frowned around his cigarette. "What are you . . . oh . . . oh shit."

He hurriedly pulled on his seat belt as Wayne shifted gears and slammed the Cherokee's gas pedal to the floor. The Cherokee lurched forward, its rear end fishtailing for just a moment on the slick street, then it gained speed rapidly and bore down on the still-slowing Cadillac.

Then there was a tremendous crash and the boys' bodies jerked against their restraints. Steve's cigarette popped out of his mouth and he let out a whoop. The Cadillac's driver lost control of his car for a wild moment and swerved across the double yellow line. Wayne downshifted and backed off as the Cadillac swung back into its proper lane and then moved over to the shoulder of the road. Wayne slowed and pulled up behind it.

The Cadillac's driver's side door popped open and a fat man in a cheap brown suit heaved himself out. The man was bald and had a pudgy pink face. He looked kind of like a human toad. He shook a fist as he approached the Cherokee, his mouth moving as he screamed words that were lost to the swirling wind.

Wayne cranked his window down and in a moment the man's pudgy face was filling that space. "You goddamn careless punks. Look what you did to my beautiful car." He waved a hand at the Cadillac. Wayne looked. The Cad's rear bumper was dented pretty badly, but he doubted he'd inflicted anything more than cosmetic damage.

Wayne shrugged and smiled. "Sorry about that, dude."

The fat man spluttered. "You . . . you . . . you're sorry? That's *it?* You worthless, rotten punk. I saw you speed up. You did that on *purpose.* What's the matter with you?"

Wayne's expression hardened. "I need you to help me with something, toady."

The fat man's eyes went wide and his face turned scarlet. "Wh-WHAT!?"

Steve snickered. "Whoa . . . dude's gonna stroke out if you're not careful, bro."

"Fuck being careful. It's time to take care of business."

"TCB, I can dig it. You and the King."

Wayne lifted the Colt .45 from his lap and pointed the barrel at the man's nose.

"Like I said, you're gonna help us with something. You're a teacher or something at the center there, right? Well, you're gonna get us in."

The man's mouth moved up and down, but no sound came out. Then his eyes rolled back, displaying only white, and he fell with a heavy thump to the cold, hard ground.

Wayne shook his head. "Lame."

He opened the door and stepped out into the rain.

Nine
Dirty Deeds Done Dirt Cheap

The door was adjacent to a large laundry room. This part of the building was where a lot of the blue collar behind-the-scenes work was done. Also housed here were the main maintenance facilities, kitchen, and a dingy break room where the lowly wage slaves dined on cheap microwave dinners and vending machine snacks. The teachers and so-called spiritual advisers rarely ventured down here, which was why Melissa was so shocked to hear Sybil Huffington's cultured voice emanating from the far end of the hallway that stretched to her left.

Her head jerked in that direction, away from the view of the staggering drunks—she assumed they were drunks—outside. The hallway ended at a wall and then branched to the left. Miss Huffington's voice was coming closer, from just around that corner. And now she heard a man's voice. She couldn't make out what was being said, but it hardly mattered. Any moment now the queen bitch of the SIMRC would step into view and she and her friends would be in a world of shit.

She seized David by a bicep and dragged him away from the door. His gaze had still been riveted to the drunks outside. He spun toward her, confusion writ large in his angular features. Then he too heard the voices.

He grimaced. "Aw, shit."

Lindy let out a squeak and hurried past Melissa, back the way they had come. Melissa followed with David in tow, but she had to wonder what the point was. They were stupid to have even tried this. There were too many obstacles and too many unforeseen complications. They were going to get caught, and in a short enough time she would again find herself at the mercy of Mark Cheney.

No.

She wouldn't let that happen, ever. She'd sooner die. And if that sick son of a bitch ever dared to whip out that tiny dick of his in her presence again, she was going to tear it off. Rip it off and feed it to him.

At the end of this stretch of hallway was a large metal door. Through that was a staircase. They could go back that way and get back to their rooms in a hurry. In theory. But it looked like Lindy had no intention of doing that. Good for her. The chick was ditzy as hell, but she had guts. They followed her through an open archway into the tiny break room. It was about the size of one of the classrooms on the third floor and was dominated by several small round tables and a number of gray metal folding chairs. Three vending machines stood against the far wall. There was nowhere to hide, except maybe under the little tables, but only a blind person would miss three teenagers huddled under those things.

David ran a hand through his wavy hair. "We're fucked."

"Maybe not."

Melissa threw herself flat against the stretch of wall just inside the archway and the others quickly followed suit. They stood very still for long moments. The hallway outside remained quiet for a time, but soon there came the click of heels on hallway tiles. The voices were audible again, though it was mostly Miss Huffington talking. Her tone was animated, verging on agitated, and for a moment Melissa was sure their escape attempt had been detected somehow. But as the voices drew closer—and as the words uttered became clearer—she realized the source of the headmistress's ire had to be something entirely unrelated to them.

"Something has to be done about the man, Gerald, and I think I'm being damned generous."

And now the man spoke, his deep voice clear for the first time. "I dunno. I don't like the bastard either, but two grand is an insult."

Melissa frowned. She turned her head to glance at David, who shrugged.

The footsteps came to an abrupt halt.

Melissa couldn't help herself.

She edged sideways a bit, turned, and peered around the edge of the archway. She knew this increased the odds of being discovered, but something within her felt compelled to find out who Miss Huffington was talking to and what they were discussing.

The guard was in the standard black and gray uniform they all wore, but Miss Huffington looked not at all like her normal self. Frowzy. Her hair was a mess and she appeared to have dressed hastily. She looked like a person who'd just jumped out of bed to tend to some emergency. And judging from her general demeanor, this was indeed the case..

"Two thousand dollars is a lot of money, Gerald. Either accept the offer or I'll find someone else to do it."

The guard snorted. "Right. He'll be here any minute, you said. You don't have time to find someone else."

Sybil Huffington's clenched fists were shaking. She clearly ached to slap the man. "You listen to me. I simply can't afford more right now. If you require an additional payment of, say, another two thousand, it will have to wait another month."

"Right. I happen to know you're not that hard up."

Sybil unclenched her hands and appeared to take a deep breath. She breathed out slowly and forced a faint smile. "So be it. I'll do it myself. I'll even drag his worthless carcass out to the woods and dig a hole for him myself."

The guard laughed. "Yeah, okay. In this weather? You? I don't think so. Listen . . . there is one more, ah . . . thing . . . you can do for me to sort of, well . . . seal the deal." He laughed again, but this time there was a nervous edge to it. "A non-monetary consideration."

Sybil's smile vanished, but she took a slow step toward him. "Yes?"

The guard coughed and ran a hand through his hair. Definitely nervous now. "Yeah, well, you know . . . I've always sort of had the hots for you, and, um . . . well . . ."

She took another step toward him. "I see. Understandable."

Then she dropped to her knees and reached for his zipper. In another moment his fly was undone and his rapidly hardening cock was in her hand. She looked up at him. "Is this what you had in mind?"

A visible shudder rippled through the guard's entire body. "Y-yes . . ."

Melissa watched with a mixture of disgust and odd fascination as the headmistress drew the man's organ into her mouth. Her breath grew short. She gripped the edge of the wall to steady herself. She wondered what was wrong with her. Maybe it was just that she'd never watched two adults engaged in a sex act in real life before. This wasn't like in the movies at all. There was no swelling music, no creative photography. Just this blunt animal act. The man's face contorted as if he was in great pain, but the sounds coming from his mouth indicated otherwise. And then, hardly more than two minutes after it had begun, the act was finished. Miss Huffington stood and wiped her mouth with the back of a hand while the still-shaking guard clumsily zipped himself up.

Melissa was stunned to realize she was shaking every bit as hard as the guard. She felt queasy. A sheen of sweat had formed on her forehead. Then she had a mental flash, like a scene from a too-vivid nightmare, except that this nightmare was real, a memory she wished she could excise from her mind forever. She was bent over Mark Cheney's desk, his heavy weight pinning her down, making the desk blotter beneath her slide every time he thrust against her. She remembered the blandness of the wall behind the desk, adorned only with a signed diploma from some southern university and a framed and autographed picture of President Ronald Reagan. She'd never be able to look at Reagan's face again without thinking of those awful moments in Cheney's office.

Miss Huffington's hand flashed, snapped across the man's cheek. "You're pathetic."

The guard rubbed his cheek. He didn't say anything.

"I trust, however, that we have come to terms."

He nodded. "Yeah. Okay."

"Good. Report to me after you've killed and disposed of Cheney."

Melissa gulped.

Holy shit!

It had sounded like they were discussing a murder-for-hire, but she had thought she must be misunderstanding what was being said. But no, they'd really been talking about killing someone. Not only that, the person they were talking about was the one person in the world she'd love to see dead.

Maybe Miss Huffington wasn't so bad after all.

Something drew Miss Huffington's gaze to the frosted glass window on the rear door. The headmistress frowned and moved to the door, bending a little at the waist to peer through the window.

Then her head snapped toward the guard. "We have intruders on the property."

The guard's hand went to the gun holstered on his belt. "I'll get rid of them."

Miss Huffington straightened. "That won't be necessary. They're weaving, barely upright. I'll shoo the drunks off. You get back to your post and intercept Cheney. Time's short."

The guard nodded, then turned and hurried away.

Miss Huffington punched the metal push bar at the door's center and stepped outside, pausing for a moment to prop the door open with a cinder block. She then disappeared into the darkness beyond the door. They heard her strident tone as she yelled at the intruders to get off the property.

David leaned close to Melissa and whispered in her ear. "What's going on? Why doesn't she just call the police to get rid of them?"

Melissa remained poised against the edge of the archway, but turned her head to look at David. "Didn't you hear them? They're gonna kill Mr. Cheney. Last thing they'll want is police around."

Lindy let out a frightened little whimper. She stepped around Melissa to get her own look at the hallway. "This is too much. I think we should just get back to our rooms while we have a chance. If they find us and figure out we heard them talking about . . ."

Lindy's voice trailed off and she whimpered again.

Melissa looked at her. The girl's eyes glistened with tears. As much as she wanted out of this place, she had to admit Lindy's suggestion was the only smart option at this point. Miss Huffington was getting rid of Cheney. That would make things more bearable for a while, give her time to plot a more efficient means of escape.

She sighed. "Okay. You're probably—"

A high, sharp scream cut her off.

Lindy emitted a startled shriek of her own and Melissa's head snapped back toward the open rear door. She saw darkness and a very faint suggestion of movement. She moved away from the archway, out into the hallway.

David put a hand on her shoulder. "Melissa, no! What are you doing?"

Melissa shrugged his hand away.

Another scream resonated in the night, this one much closer. Then Sybil Huffington came stumbling through the open door, collapsing to the tiled floor in a shuddering, whimpering heap. Melissa let her bag slide off her shoulder and drop to the floor. She took a few tentative steps toward the fallen headmistress. She shouldn't be doing this, should only be worried about saving her own skin, but she couldn't help it. The woman was in trouble. She needed help. David and Lindy reluctantly followed her into the hallway.

Sybil Huffington raised her head and blinked at them in confusion. "What are you children doing out of your rooms?" Melissa's mouth opened. Her jaw worked, but no sound came out. Never mind, I don't want to know."

Sybil got to her knees and Melissa saw that the woman's blouse had been shredded across the front. Blood oozed in trickles from the tatters. More blood welled from a wound on her forearm. It almost looked as if she'd been . . . bitten.

Melissa thought about the drunks she'd seen out back.

Had they done that?

Sybil extended a hand toward them. "Someone help me. There's crazy people outside. Dangerous people." She glanced behind her. "We need to get that door closed."

David sprang into motion then, stepping past the headmistress while Melissa took her hand and helped the woman to her feet. Sybil squeezed her hand tight, almost too tight. She stared into Melissa's eyes, her own eyes projecting a coldness that made Melissa shiver. "Is it just the three of you down here?"

Melissa's lower lip trembled. "I . . . I . . ."

Melissa was scared shitless. This was a woman who'd just negotiated the price of a man's murder the way other people might haggle over the price of a car (except for the blowjob). She wasn't dumb. She would know they'd been hiding out nearby, had probably heard every word of her conversation with the guard.

She wouldn't be able to let them live.

Melissa tried to twist out of the woman's grip, but the headmistress was stronger and easily held on. "You'll not be going anywhere, dear." Something subtle shifted in her features then. A hint of a leer. Strange. "Your friends will spend the night in isolation rooms, and you will accompany me to my office."

Melissa felt something wet on her hand. She glanced down and saw that blood from Miss Huffington's arm wound on her wrist. Blood was still flowing at a pretty good rate from that wound. What the hell? That had to hurt like a motherfucker. Maybe adrenaline was blunting the pain. Whatever the case, she realized something in that moment.

Miss Huffington wasn't just a woman capable of murder.

She was stone cold crazy.

She tried again to twist free.

Miss Huffington clamped her free hand around Melissa's neck, squeezing hard.

The scream that came then startled both of them. Miss Huffington released Melissa and spun toward the door. David stumbled backward through the door, tripped, and landed hard on his back. Melissa loosed a scream of her own as the first of the "drunks" came staggering through the door.

Melissa recognized the girl.

Anna Kincaid.

And she recognized something else.

Anna was dead.

Dead, but upright—and intent on nothing but bloody murder.

Her eyes were empty and glassy, her mouth rimmed with blood and flecks of what looked like raw meat. Her mouth opened and a sound like the low warning snarl of a Rottweiler emanated from her throat.

Lindy said, "Ohmigod! She's a zombie!"

A zombie, Melissa thought, mind going numb. *That's not possible.*

David began to scoot backward, but Anna fell upon him, her open, blood-encrusted mouth diving toward his neck before he could twist away. Her teeth punched into his throat, dug deep, and blood spurted in a high, red arc as she wrenched her head away.

Melissa's legs went weak and she stumbled sideways, falling against the wall.

Lindy fell against her, clutching at her, buried her face in her neck as she mewled like a baby.

More zombies lurched through the still open door. Two were dressed like hookers, their decaying bodies dripping with dirt. The stench of rot filled the air.

A dead man followed them through the door.

Quigley, the maintenance man.

Now it was Sybil Huffington's turn to scream.

She turned and bolted toward the staircase at the end of the hallway, leaving Melissa and Lindy to fend for themselves.

Ten
Gimme Gimme
Shock Treatment

Wayne was acutely aware of the need to get the fat man up and mobile again before some well-meaning motorist stopped and offered to lend a helping hand. Or worse yet, a cop. A showdown with the law armed only with an unloaded handgun couldn't end well.

The Cherokee's passenger door creaked open and in a moment he heard the crunch of booted feet on gravel. He looked up and saw Steve peering down at the unconscious man. Rain flattened his teased-out hair, making his long, lean figure vaguely resemble a wilted scarecrow.

"Is this dude dead?"

Wayne looked at the man's chest, saw it rise a little, then fall again. "No, thank God. But we've got to get him up and inside that fucking Caddy soon."

"Yeah." Steve lifted his head and looked first to his left and then to his right, searching the road for approaching cars. "Have you tried slapping him?"

"Yeah."

"And?"

Wayne made an exasperated sound. "Nothing. Like slapping a bowling ball."

"Well, shit."

Steve knelt at the opposite side of the man's body and lifted one of his thick arms, slid a hand under a damp armpit. He indicated the man's other arm with a nod. "We're gonna have to drag him."

Wayne groaned. "Fuck. Dude has to weigh three-hundred pounds."

"Yeah, so the sooner we get started, the better."

Wayne resigned himself to the task. Dragging hundreds of pounds of dead weight across a rain-slicked road was a job better suited to Arnold Schwarzenegger or some other weight-lifting son of a bitch. Wayne was no Schwarzenegger. He was a skinny kid from the suburbs. The bulk of his exercise came from manipulating an Atari joystick. But there was nothing for it but to do it. He shoved the empty .45 into the waistband of his wet jeans and got a grip on the man's other arm.

Steve looked him in the eye. "Ready?"

Wayne nodded. "Yeah."

"Count of three, then. One, two—"

Wayne got his feet planted solidly beneath him and pushed backward with everything he had as Steve reached the end of the count-off. The body slid a good two feet across the road's shoulder. Getting started was the hard part. The rest of it was just a matter of keeping focused and bearing down. His shoulders were aching by the time they reached the Cad's open driver's side door. And he felt as if someone had clubbed him in the small of the back with a heavy wrench. But they'd reached their destination and still the road in both directions remained dark. Yet they couldn't afford to rest—their luck couldn't hold out forever.

They hoisted the unconscious man to a sitting position. Steve hurried to the other side of the car, opened the door there and crawled across the front seat. He reached beneath the seat, found a lever, and pushed the seat back. He then slipped his hands beneath the man's armpits and looked at Wayne. "I'll pull, you push."

Wayne grimaced. "Goddamn. You'd think he'd wake up."

"Oh, he's gonna wake up, one way or another. Let's do this."

Wayne dropped to his knees, got his feet planted behind him, and reached between the man's legs to get a solid grip on the backs of his prodigious thighs. He signaled readiness and Steve did the count-off again. Steve provided enough of an initial lift so that Wayne was

51

able to really put his shoulder into it. The man's torso came off the wet gravel and in a few more moments they had him wedged behind the steering wheel. They spent a few more moments getting his legs situated in the well beneath the steering wheel. Then Wayne threw the door shut, opened the rear door, and slid into the back seat.

Steve peered at him over the top of the front seat. "I'll be right back, dude. Gonna get my gun and close up your ride."

"Get my keys, too."

"Right."

Then he was gone and Wayne was alone in the car with the SIMRC man. He removed the .45 from his waistband and leaned over the front seat to study the man's puffy face His head lolled to one side, mouth hanging open, a small pink wedge of tongue visible between the lips. He wondered about the man, whether he was a part of the center's administrative team or instead played some active role in the brainwashing of supposedly wayward children. Not that it mattered. He clearly worked there, and therefore, as far as Wayne was concerned, was guilty by association of whatever horrible thing was happening to Melissa.

The car shook slightly as the front passenger door was yanked open and Steve plopped back inside. Steve passed him his keys and pulled the door shut. He then showed Wayne an expression far more solemn than he was used to seeing from his friend.

"Here's where we go hardcore, dude."

He punched in the Cad's cigarette lighter.

Steve's eyes widened. "Oh. Um . . . I don't know about this, dude."

"What do you mean?

Wayne blinked. "You're gonna threaten him with that, right? With torture?"

Steve rolled his eyes. "Torture? Yeah, if you wanna get technical about it. You got any better ideas? You could try slapping him again."

Wayne tried it.

The man still didn't stir.

"It's like he's in a fuckin' coma."

"Maybe he had a stroke or something when you pointed that .45 at him."

Wayne's face pinched up. "Shit, don't say that."

The cigarette lighter popped out and Steve removed the little cylinder from its circular slot on the dash. The end glowed bright red in the semi-darkness. Wayne's stomach tightened as he watched his friend apply those red-hot coils to the back of the man's right hand. Bile rose in his throat at the sound of the flesh sizzling, and the smell of burning meat made his eyes water. A few seconds passed, and he began to think Steve's guess about a stroke had been on the mark. Then the man jerked awake with a high-pitched gasp and yanked his hand away from the lighter. He made blubbering sounds and held his hand up to gape stupidly at the seared flesh. Though he was in great pain, he seemed disoriented for several more moments. Then awareness returned. The man saw that he was in his own car again, and with him were the two hooligans who'd rammed him from behind.

He groped for the door handle.

Wayne pointed the .45 at the man's face and prayed the asshole wouldn't faint again.

"Don't."

The single terse syllable was enough to still the man's hand. His eyes filled with tears and he began to blubber again. "Oh, please . . . please . . . oh, don't kill me. Oh, please . . ."

Steve waved the still-glowing lighter at him and the man cowered against the door. "Shut up with the whining, you big pussy. We need you to concentrate and listen up."

The man's eyes danced in their sockets, flicking back and forth, unable to focus for more than a second solely on the .45 or the lighter. The big roll of flesh beneath his chin jiggled. He was breathing in rapid gasps, and Wayne feared he was on the verge of hyperventilating. But then he seemed to relax some. The man wasn't an idiot. He drove a nice Caddy and wore a suit. He was an asshole, but an at least moderately successful one. Which meant he would be the kind of man who would eventually stop freaking out and start focusing on what he needed to do to extricate himself from this situation.

Or so Wayne hoped.

If not, they'd have to figure something else out. Maybe go into full-on commando mode. Knock this guy out and stuff him in the trunk. Then ram the Caddy through the gated entrance and use the unloaded guns to bluff their way past the security dudes. He really hoped it wouldn't come to that. Every time he considered that option his stomach started tying itself in knots. He tried to picture it and could only imagine the security guards laughing at him before taking his gun away.

But their captive did manage to compose himself, after taking several deep breaths.

Wayne forced back a sigh of relief. Perception mattered. He didn't want this guy to see any hint of how non-hardcore they were not so far beneath the surface.

"What do you punks want from me?"

Wayne told him.

The man stared at them for several moments after he'd finished laying it out for him, his expression blank. Then his wormy lips curled in a smarmy smile. "You morons. Do you actually believe this will work?"

Steve smirked. "It better work, motherfucker."

Now the man's expression mirrored Steve's, with perhaps an additional measure of arrogance. "Or what?"

Steve held his gaze for a moment, didn't say anything at first. His expression went blank, his eyes flat and cold. Wayne began to wonder if maybe his friend really did have some kind of genuine badass potential lurking within him. Right now he looked like Clint Eastwood in one of those spaghetti westerns. A cold motherfucker. A dude you knew you'd never wanna fuck with after just one look in the eyes. His expression didn't change as he returned the lighter to its slot in the dashboard. Nor did it change when he withdrew from a jacket pocket the gun Wayne had given him earlier.

And it didn't change when he jabbed the barrel of the gun into the man's big belly, pressing hard, really leaning into it. "You're gonna do it, man. And you're gonna deliver the performance of your life. I know this because this here gun's gonna be on you the whole time. And the second I think you're fucking us, I'm gonna pull the trigger and blow a big fucking hole through your gut." The corners of his mouth tilted upward in the smallest, coldest smile Wayne had ever seen. "You dig me, man?"

The man was panting again. Wayne figured he wasn't far from tipping back into total freakout mode. But he swallowed hard and managed to croak out a single word: "Okay."

Steve eased up on him, removing the gun from the man's belly and returning to his side of the seat. His smile broadened some, but his eyes remained cold. "Cool." He looked at Wayne. "See that? You have to be firm with 'em, man, get 'em to chill. That way we don't wind up having to blast a bunch of motherfuckers like when we robbed that bank in Cleveland."

Wayne pursed his lips hard. Dammit. Rob a bank in Cleveland?

I'm not gonna laugh, he thought. *No fuckin' way.*

Somehow he managed to contain the burst of mad laughter swelling within him. But it was a close call. Luckily, the man's attention had remained on Steve the whole time. If he knew or suspected Steve's bank robbery ad-lib was fiction, he gave no indication of it.

He cleared his throat and sat up straighter in his seat. "We're going to need a cover story. Something to explain why you boys are with me."

Wayne had already given that some thought. "We're brothers. An out-of-control juvenile delinquent duo. You're bringing us in tonight as a personal favor to our parents, who are old friends of yours. You'll process us through the proper channels tomorrow, but our parents want us off the streets as soon as possible, so you're gonna get us situated in a room or cell or whatever tonight."

The man's brow creased and his fat bottom lip pushed out as he thought about it. "Hmm." He made an odd sound in his throat and shook his head. "Dear God, that just might work."

Steve cackled. "You're a genius, bro."

The man rubbed his chin and nodded. "You'll need names, though."

Wayne frowned. "Huh?"

"Names. We'll need to sign you in at the gatehouse. Because you clearly intend to commit some heinous crime once you're inside the building, I assume you will not wish to use your birth names."

Wayne thought about it a moment, then a slow grin tugged at the edges of his mouth. "We're Angus and Malcolm Young. I'll be Angus."

Steve snickered. "You'll be anus."

"Shut up, dude."

The man sighed, clearly not amused. Not an AC/DC fan, apparently. "That should be fine." Then his eyes narrowed and his brow creased again. "I may well succeed in getting you inside the center. Do I really want to know what you have in mind once that's accomplished?"

Wayne shrugged. "We're rescuing my girlfriend."

"I see. Might I ask her name?"

"Melissa Campbell."

Something flared in the man's eyes then. A corner of his mouth twitched twice. He shifted his bulk behind the steering wheel. Wayne peered more intently at him. How strange. But there could be no doubt about it. The man was visibly more nervous than he'd been a moment ago. Wayne was tempted to dismiss the man's sudden twitchiness as mere coincidence, but his girlfriend was in trouble. Something bad had happened to her here. It wasn't beyond the realm of possibility that this man was responsible. His hand tightened around the .45's grip. He was tempted to bust the man's skull open with the butt of the gun.

But he drew in a deep breath, made himself calm down.

He didn't know anything yet, not really. Gut instinct wasn't enough to go on. The main thing now was to keep it together and get into the center. Then they'd find their way to Melissa, and at that point they'd find out the truth.

He tapped the back of the man's head with the .45. "What's your name, old dude?"

The man winced at the touch of cold steel on his bald scalp. "Cheney. Mark Cheney."

"Okay, Mark Cheney. Enough fucking around. Let's do this."

Wayne settled back in his seat and tucked the .45 beneath a flap of his jacket. Mark Cheney shifted in his seat again, reached for the key that was still in the ignition, gave it a twist, and the luxury car's big engine came to life with a rumbling purr. He shifted gears and tapped the gas pedal. Moments later they were headed down the winding driveway leading to the Southern Illinois Music Re-Education Center.

Eleven
Personality Crisis

The pain finally began to make its presence known as she made the second floor landing. Sybil Huffington grimaced and fell against the staircase wall. She let out a whimper and held up her right forearm for a closer inspection. A hunk of flesh there had been torn out by the thing she had belatedly realized was Anna Kincaid, somehow reanimated and transformed into a drooling, vacant-eyed cannibal. Never mind how that could possibly have happened. She didn't have time to theorize. All that mattered was getting her precious ass the hell out of harm's way just as fast as she could.

She calmed some as she studied the wound. Though it looked awful, was, in fact, a bloody mess, the damage wasn't lethal. She needed to clean and disinfect it, then get a bandage on it, and the sooner the better. But it wasn't going to kill her. She lifted her tattered blouse and saw that the wounds there were superficial. Just scratches Before taking a bite out of her arm, Anna had taken a swipe at her with an outstretched hand, her long nails shredding the fabric with talon-like ease. The dead girl's display of strength had shocked her, and she'd stood there like the proverbial deer trapped in headlights as the girl seized her arm and took a bite out of it. At that point survival instinct kicked in, a hot shot of adrenaline hitting her veins as she twisted free of the dead girl's grip and began her retreat. But she'd gotten a look at the resurrected hookers before turning to run. Still decked-out in slut-for-hire threads, but otherwise looking like extras from the set of a cheap horror movie.

Madness.

These were the women she'd murdered in her office, of that there could be no doubt. She shivered and turned to hug the wall, her trembling hands clawing pathetically at the painted concrete. The sudden conviction that what was happening was a judgment from God made her whimper. Who else but God possessed the power to resurrect the dead?

The pitiless religious beliefs she'd privately rejected years ago surged to the forefront of consciousness. Clearly this was *His* will.

Just as clear was a single stark fact—she was fucked.

She stood shaking against the wall for another long moment. Then she heard faint screams from the first floor hallway. The closed door below muffled the sound, but the terror felt by the girls she'd left behind was clear enough. Mingled with the screams was the even fainter sound of some commotion. She heard a crash, followed by what might have been the sound of breaking glass.

A strange thing happened then—the sense of panic gripping her eased . . . then released her.

And she smiled.

Because she'd realized something. Perhaps it was true that God had set this macabre series of events into motion. It was even possible this was some form of judgment against her. That did not, however, mean she was doomed. She could survive this, but doing so would mean keeping her wits about her and finding within her the will to do what needed to be done. Okay, so God had resurrected her victims and sent them against her. They were His instrument. Wasn't it possible this was something more than a judgment?

What if it was a test?

Yes.

If she somehow managed to survive this night, perhaps she would be redeemed in the eyes of God. It was a stretch. A big one. And she knew it. But it was the only thread of hope available to her and she meant to cling to it as long as there was breath left in her body.

To survive the trial, she would need to destroy God's instrument.

Kill Anna and the hookers.

Again. Preferably in a more permanent manner this time.

Oh, and she'd have to kill Quigley. And those girls. And Gerald, the Neanderthal guard whose semen she could still taste in her mouth, preferably after he'd already taken care of Mark Cheney for her. Lord, but there was a lot of killing to be done. Of course, it wasn't without precedent. She thought back to stories from the bible, to the tales of bloody, terrible sacrifice. And the tiny spark of hope flared brighter as she thought of another angle. The girls and women she'd killed shared one very significant thing in common.

They were sinners.

So maybe she had it all wrong.

Perhaps *she* was the lord's instrument, a means by which He could punish some of those who had transgressed against Him.

Yes!

It was so clear to her now. It was no accident of fate that she had wound up in this place. Her career, her position of power at the SIMRC, was part of a predetermined plan, the end destination of a path she'd been set upon at birth. The center was a veritable warehouse of sin, the boys and girls housed here tainted in the eyes of their Creator. And it had been her sacred duty to cleanse them of that taint. Some, of course, could not be cleansed, their sinning ways as intractable as a skid row bum's alcoholism. Anna Kincaid, for example. Killing those that were beyond saving had merely been another necessary part of her holy duty. That she had derived what many might view as "perverse" pleasures from the punishments she'd meted out was unimportant. She understood now that these pleasures had been her earthly reward for carrying out His will.

And what a glorious reward it had been.

Alas, the time had come to move on.

Thus fortified by rationalization, Sybil pushed herself away from the wall and stepped toward the door to the second floor. A fresh round of screams emanated from the hallway below, but she ignored them. With any luck, the zombies would kill the girls, eliminating one small but important piece of the puzzle facing her. The thing she had to do now was get back to the other side of the building, back to her office and adjacent apartment. She would be safe from the developing chaos there and would have a chance to collect her wits and better assess her next steps.

She opened the door, saw only gleaming tiles and a row of closed doors to either side, and took off at a run. A little gasp escaped her throat as the world slipped out from under her.

The following occurred in less than the space of a second:

A glimpse of white ceiling above her.

An awareness that she was falling *away* from the ceiling.

Then—impact, the hard smack of floor tiles against the crown of her skull.

Fuzzy moments passed. At first there was numbness. Then pain, and a lot of it. Her neck felt . . . wrong. She tried to lift her head and the pain ratcheted up, shot spikes of agony through her shoulders and down her spine. Several feet ahead of her, propped open on the floor, was a yellow CAUTION WET FLOOR sign.

Her head dipped backward.

Her vision blurred.

She understood she was badly injured and might be dying—and then knew a moment of utter, blinding terror at possibly being within moments of facing God's true and final judgment.

Somewhere nearby a door opened.

Voices in the hallway. One male, one female.

A face loomed over her, a pretty girl. Young.

The face was grinning.

Sybil Huffington blacked out.

61

Twelve
Pretty Baby Scream

Lindy's frantic screams reverberated in the hallway. The screams were punctuated by desperate, wailing pleas for help. But Melissa was too busy fending off one of the dead hookers to help her. The thing's eyes were gone and its flesh showed some evidence of decomposition, but it still had some meat on its bones and so looked less like a walking skeleton than the other zombie whore. Its legs still looked shapely encased in tattered fishnet stockings, while its largish breasts strained the filthy fabric of a skimpy top. She was a necrophiliac's wet dream come true.

The zombie had her pinned against the edge of the break room's archway. Melissa's forearm was jammed up under the dead thing's jaw, every ounce of strength she possessed going into the effort to keep its questing mouth away from her face. With her free hand she swatted at the zombie's groping hands, but several times its long nails gouged and scratched her flesh, shredding her clothes in the process. Her only advantage at this point was the zombie's sheer stupidity. God help her if it ever thought to draw its head back and take a bite out of her arm.

She tried again to use her legs against the thing, but the zombie's closeness and unnatural level of strength prevented her from achieving the leverage necessary to deliver a kick or knee to the midsection. She couldn't even stomp on its feet.

Lindy screamed again. This time the sound was higher and louder than before. She'd been hurt. Melissa jerked her head to the right and saw the other girl grappling with both Anna Kincaid and the more rotted of the dead hookers. She was in the break room, where she had been circling the tables to keep her distance from the zombies. The tactic had worked for a while, but Anna and the hooker had finally managed to flank her. Now she was using one of the metal folding chairs as a shield. They had driven her into a corner of the room, but she was keeping them at bay by pushing them back with the chair each time they advanced. She was fighting hard, but she couldn't hold them back much longer.

Melissa's own strength began to ebb and her forearm slipped.

The zombie's mouth dove toward her suddenly exposed neck.

Melissa shifted her weight and lurched hard to her left. The move came at the exact right time. The zombie was off balance. They fell in a tangled heap to the floor. She kicked and thrashed her way free of the zombie's embrace. Its fingernails raked at her arms as she rose, etching scarlet lines in pale flesh. Melissa backpedaled and found herself standing in the hallway. The zombie she'd just fought off was still on its back on the floor. Now it rolled stiffly to its side and began the laborious process of getting upright again.

Melissa glanced left and right.

To her left was an empty hallway and an open door. Well, not quite empty. David's corpse was still sprawled on the floor amidst a wide pool of dark blood. To her right, the hallway dead-ended. There was another door there, the one through which Miss Huffington had disappeared, but it was closed. The dead maintenance man was at that door, face pressed against the window, his right hand pawing clumsily at the doorknob.

She faced a hard choice.

She could escape through the open door now.

Or she could help Lindy.

The girl's tenacity was amazing and admirable, worthy of any soldier in combat. But she was just one girl. There were three zombies in the break room. The math was pretty simple. Abandoning Lindy now would be tantamount to sentencing her to death. Melissa wasn't sure she could live with that. Even so, it was a tough call. She didn't want to die. Nor did she wish to fight any more.

A flicker of movement to her left drew her attention back that way.

David was on his knees. The gaping wound in his neck had stopped leaking blood. He looked at her with empty eyes. Eyes devoid of recognition. Her friend was one of them now. A zombie. David's mouth opened and a hissing moan escaped his throat. He staggered to his feet as she watched and began to lurch toward her.

Melissa sighed.

The decision had been made for her.

She stepped back into the break room. The zombie hooker was on its knees now. It saw Melissa coming and opened its mouth in a hungry snarl. Melissa moved in fast, delivering a hard kick to the creature's concave abdomen. It flopped onto its back again and Melissa sidestepped its outreached hands.

Lindy continued to fight off Anna and the other hooker. They were getting closer between swats from the folding chair, advancing inch by inch, oblivious to any pain from the heavy blows. Soon she wouldn't have room to swing the chair and then it'd be all over for Lindy. Melissa considered using another folding chair to mount a rear assault. If she could draw just one of them away, Lindy could slip out of that damn corner.

She scanned the room for a more formidable weapon and her gaze locked on the counter set against the wall to her left. She saw a sink. A coffee maker. A basket filled with napkins and condiments. A row of cabinets above. A row of drawers below. Her heart raced. The zombie on the floor started to get up again. She ignored it and hurried over to the counter. She yanked open a drawer and found an old telephone book and a small stack of magazines. She threw it shut and opened the next drawer.

Bingo.

A cutlery tray loaded with gleaming spoons, forks, and knives.

Including one very long—and very sharp—carving knife.

She grabbed it and advanced on the zombies in the corner. Lindy saw what she was doing and paused between swats, eyes going wide with hope. Anna Kincaid took advantage of the momentary lapse, charging Lindy and getting past the chair. Lindy screamed and grappled with the dead girl, holding the zombie's head back with a hand braced beneath its chin. One of her fingers slipped between Anna's lips and the zombie bit down instantly. Lindy screamed and thrashed. Her hand came away from Anna's mouth with two fingers missing, blood spurting from the ragged stumps. All of this happened in the space of maybe a second. In the next second, Melissa adjusted her grip on the carving knife's handle and swung it in a vicious arc toward Zombie Whore 2's head. The point of the blade punched into its temple then slammed into whatever was left of its brain.

The zombie jerked and went rigid.

Melissa yanked the knife out of its head and it toppled to the floor. Dead again.

And Melissa thought, *Just like in the movies.*

Kill the brain to kill the zombie.

Lindy was still fighting, despite the enormous pain she must be suffering. Her good hand was locked around Anna's throat, with her arm fully extended, keeping the thing's blood-flecked mouth well away. Blood still flowed freely from those finger stumps, though. All the willpower in the world wouldn't save her if she lost too much blood.

Melissa raised the knife again and moved to help her.

Then she heard something to her rear and turned to see Zombie Whore 1 coming at her again. Its mouth was open, lips stretched wide in a hungry expression that looked disturbingly like a mocking grin.

And it wasn't alone.

David was a few feet behind her, arms outstretched, teeth bared.

Melissa thought, *I am so fucked.*

Then she heard distant voices, adult male voices. Guards, maybe. Moments later she heard the sound of approaching feet.

Then voices again, distinct now.

"Holy mother . . . look at all the fucking blood!"

Another voice: "What the . . . is that Quigley? Hey, Quigley!"

Lindy screamed again and that brought the men running into the break room, where they pulled up short at the sight of the carnage. All that blood in the corner. A nasty-looking corpse on the floor. Two badly messed-up people advancing on a girl holding a bloody knife.

One of the men pulled a gun and aimed it at Melissa's head.

"Put the fucking knife down, bitch!"

Melissa sighed. *Idiots.*

The zombies were still coming at her, greedy hands reaching for her. And these geniuses thought *she* was the threat?

Jesus wept.

Quigley appeared behind them, head down, drool depending from each corner of his mouth, empty eyes looking at the guard with the drawn gun. Melissa opened her mouth to shout a warning, but it was too late. The dead maintenance man took a bite out of the guard's shoulder.

The guard shrieked.

His trigger finger squeezed reflexively.

The blast was hugely loud in the little break room.

Another scream rang out and a body fell to the floor.

Thirteen
Raining Blood

Something was happening. Something was wrong.

That much was apparent the moment the Cadillac rolled up to the gatehouse. The so-called "gatehouse" was actually just a booth with waist-high windows on every side. The "gate" was a plank mounted on a stanchion at the rear of the booth. A flick of a switch would cause it to raise up or down. Wayne had imagined something much more elaborate. A metal gate, for starters, and maybe a high chain-link fence tipped with coils of barbed wire. Armed guards with rifles patrolling the perimeter. Frothing guard dogs straining at leashes.

But the low-key security made sense, now that he thought about it. The SIMRC wasn't the state pen. Rather, it was a kind of alternative school, albeit one teaching an insidious doctrine of blind faith in the value of conformity. Most of the "students" were here against their will, but they weren't prisoners. Not really.

At least that was the official party line.

There was an ugly truth behind the benign veneer, and Wayne hoped one day places like this would be widely viewed as the abominations they were.

The guard manning the booth was standing half-in and half-out of it, watching them as he spoke into a walkie talkie. He stepped out of the booth and held up a hand for them to wait. Mark Cheney responded with a nod and a wave, and the guard moved away from the Cadillac, stopping at the gate to stare at the main SIMRC building as he continued to jaw at the walkie talkie.

Wayne frowned.

The guard gestured wildly with his free hand and grimaced

several times as he listened to static-filled squawks from the walkie talkie. At one point he glanced over his shoulder at the Cadillac. He frowned and shook his head, said something else into the walkie talkie. Wayne wished he could read lips. The guy was afraid, stressed out by something. But by what?

Wayne kicked the seat in front of him. "Yo. Cheney. What's happening?"

"I . . . don't know. This is . . . unusual. Something isn't right."

Steve snorted. "No shit. If by something you mean everything about this shithole."

Cheney said, "We do good work here."

It sounded rote, like something said automatically any time someone from the outside criticized the center. Maybe he was wrong, but to Wayne's ears the words didn't resonate with the clear, bedrock faith of a true believer. The impression meshed with his belief that these people were little more than modern snake oil salesmen. Opportunists who had identified a void in the marketplace, a means of exploiting the fears of parents with troublesome children.

Fucking leeches on society's ass.

Steve scowled at Cheney. "Bullshit. You're Big Brother. This shit is 1984 three years late. The rebirth of the Third fucking Reich. You mind-controlling sons of bitches can all eat me."

Wayne wanted to tell his friend not to get so worked up, but it was too late—his outburst had drawn the attention of the guard, who turned fully toward them now and frowned again as he watched the emphatic hand gestures Steve made as he spoke. The guard spoke into the walkie talkie one more time, then lowered it and approached the Cadillac.

Cheney pushed a button and his window whirred down.

The guard knelt and peered through the open window, his gaze sweeping over the front and back seats before he spoke. Wayne locked eyes with the man for a moment and felt his stomach roll. He willed himself to remain calm, to sit tight and show no outward signs of nervousness. There were still so many ways everything could go wrong. It would suck to blow it now after having come so far. He thought of Melissa and forced his mouth to form a small smile.

The guard nodded and looked at Cheney. "Mr. Cheney, my apologies. I'm afraid I can't admit you to the facility tonight."

"But that's absurd, Gerald." Cheney spat the words out, sounding every bit like an entitled official accustomed to getting his way. Good. It meant he was still focused. And still conscious of the hidden guns pointed at him. "I spoke with Miss Huffington less than half an hour ago. She assured me I would be admitted."

The guard sighed. "I received her instructions." A corner of his mouth twitched. Wayne frowned. It looked like the man was trying not to smirk. Strange. "But circumstances have changed. We have a developing situation inside the center. Until the danger has passed, I can't let anyone in."

Danger?

The thought of Melissa facing some unknown threat overrode his better judgment. He leaned over the seat and looked the guard in the eye again. "What the fuck's going on in there, man?"

The guard's eyes narrowed.

Oh, fuck . . .

Wayne knew he was teetering on the brink of a bad mistake. But he didn't care. Melissa's safety was all that mattered. He slipped a hand inside his jacket, gripped the butt of the .45 sticking out of the inner pocket. Too bad it wasn't loaded. He felt stupid. His early notions of how this would work seemed naïve as hell now.

The guard looked at Cheney again. "What's the deal with the kids? Who are they?"

Cheney ignored the questions. "I demand to know what's happening inside the center. Answer me now if you value your job."

The guard regarded Cheney coolly for a moment before answering. "We've got a small riot of sorts going on. Hard to tell what's really happening from the scattered reports I'm getting. So you can see why it would be wise not to enter the facility at this time."

Steve blurted it out: "A fucking riot!? Are you shitting me?"

Wayne groaned.

One of guard's hands drifted to the butt of his holstered handgun. "Something's fishy here. Everyone out of the car." He drew the gun and stepped back a few paces. Now!"

Cheney opened his door and stepped out immediately. Steve threw a glance Wayne's way and shrugged. What could he do? He got out of the car and began to move toward the other side.

"Keep your hands where I can see them!" The guard raised the gun and aimed it at the center of Steve's chest. "That's right, lace your fingers behind your head, then come on over, nice and slow."

Steve did as instructed, but with a typical expression of amused insolence. "Whoa. Hold on there, Lone Ranger. No need to get excited."

"Shut your mouth, punk." He looked at the car, saw Wayne still sitting there in the back seat, and gestured with the gun. "Are you deaf, son? Get out of the car and keep your hands where I can see them."

Hopelessness settled in Wayne's gut like a lead weight. His worst fears were coming true. They had botched the mission. Melissa would never get out of this place, and he and Steve were going to jail. Then he had a thought. A crazy idea. A small smile dimpled the corners of his mouth. Hell. What he had in mind was beyond crazy. It was dangerous.

To understate.

But he was fucked anyway. Might as well go for it.

He got out of the car and saw that Cheney's big body was shielding him from the guard. Perfect. He pulled the .45, moved into position directly behind him, and aimed the gun at the back of his head. "Drop the gun, asshole, or this motherfucker's brains are gonna fly."

The guard gaped at him, disbelief etched in his features. Then he smiled and swung his own gun toward Cheney. He said one word, a seeming mockery of Wayne's own thoughts: "Perfect."

Instinct caused Wayne to lurch away from Cheney, which was good, because in the next instant the guard squeezed off a shot and a large caliber slug penetrated Cheney's forehead. The force of the blast slapped the man backward as the back of his head exploded. Brains flew. A spray of blood spattered the driveway. The dead man fell against the car, then toppled to the ground.

Steve said, "Holy shit."

Wayne's mind reeled. Fucking hell. He'd just watched a man die. Had just witnessed a cold-blooded murder. It made no sense. He felt sick. In the space of just a few seconds the world as he'd understood it had ceased to exist. All bets were off now. Any damn thing could happen. He looked at Cheney. The rain had slowed to a steady drizzle. Moisture mingled with the blood leaking from the hole in his forehead and spread a thin red film over his face.

"Drop the gun, son."

He looked at the guard. The man was aiming his weapon at him now. Wayne stared into the dark barrel and felt the lethal potential there like a weight pressing against him. He experienced a moment of perfect and profound awareness, pure knowledge of precisely how fragile and vulnerable the human body could be. He'd never felt so afraid. He didn't want to die. Didn't want to be shot.

The guard was shouting at him again.

Wayne's right hand still clutched the .45. It was aimed in the guard's general direction. Of course, the man couldn't know it wasn't loaded.

Wayne sighed.

There was really only one thing to do at this point.

It's like a card game, he thought. *Your opponent doesn't know you're holding a losing hand.*

So bluff.

He forced a sneer, invested it with phony arrogance.

He cocked the .45's hammer. Dramatic effect. "No. You drop your gun."

The guard blinked. The sound of the .45's hammer cocking had gotten to him, but he wasn't backing down yet. "Not a chance, son.

You don't have the balls. I can see that plain as the zits on your face."

A long, silent moment elapsed.

Lethal intent burned in the guard's fierce gaze. Wayne knew this showdown was seconds away from ending with him flat on his back on the wet asphalt, bleeding out from a hole in his gut. But then another ominous metallic click broke the silence.

"Do what the man said, pig. Put the fucking gun down or you're dead."

Wayne glanced at Steve and grinned. His friend had pulled the Walther and was aiming it at the guard's head. Two empty weapons pointed at a man wielding live ammo. Double bluff.

The guard froze. His jawline quivered slightly. He was afraid now.

Wayne forced a chuckle. "I were you, man, I'd do it. Guy's stone crazy. Saw him blast his way through a crowd of civilians in Cleveland not too long ago. Besides, it's two against one. You might get one of us, but you'd wind up full of holes and dead on the ground."

The guard hesitated a moment longer. A gleam in his eyes hinted at an internal war. Probably he was imagining the devastating results of all that theoretical lead pumping through his flesh. Wayne held his aim steady and prayed the man would arrive at the only sensible conclusion given the circumstances.

The guard sighed and thumbed a switch on the automatic pistol.

The safety, Wayne realized. He gestured with the .45 again. "On the ground."

The guard dropped the gun and laced his fingers behind his head. "You brats are in over your heads." The son of a bitch. He'd surrendered his weapon, but remained smug as hell.

It was irksome.

Steve took a few quick steps toward the man, raised the Walther, and slammed the butt of it against the back of the man's head. The guard let out a sharp cry and his knees buckled. His hands came away from the back of his head as he stumbled forward a step. Steve raised the Walther again. Slammed it down again. Wayne winced as it cracked against the base of the man's skull. The guard dropped to his knees with a heavy grunt, then toppled over, apparently unconscious.

Wayne swallowed with difficulty, the lump in his throat going down like a cork ball lined with razor blades. He felt sick again. "Holy . . . shit . . . . Is he dead? Did you kill him, man?"

Steve knelt next to the guard and removed a pair of handcuffs from the man's belt. He tossed the Walther aside. It hit the ground and skittered across several feet of asphalt. Wayne knew he should retrieve it. It was his dad's property. But he felt woozy, stunned by the violence of the last few minutes..

Steve wrenched the guard's hands behind his back and secured them with the handcuffs. "Dude's not dead, bro. Don't sweat it. Can hear him breathing. *Should* kill him, though. Man's a fucking psycho. You saw him shoot tubby."

"Yeah."

Like he could forget that.

"That was some fucked-up shit. Wonder why he did it."

Steve shrugged. "Who the fuck knows? He's a psycho. Psychos do psychotic shit."

Wayne nodded. You couldn't argue with logic like that.

Steve scooped up the guard's discarded gun. So that was why he'd ditched the Walther. Now he was packing heat for real. Steve tucked the gun in his waistband and grabbed hold of the guard's ankles. "Let's do this quick and get on the show."

Wayne frowned. "Do *what* quick?"

"Move these fuckers out of plain view. You gonna help me or what?"

"Yeah."

They went to work and in a few minutes they'd managed to stash the corpse and the unconscious guard in the gatehouse.

When it was done, Wayne stood panting against the booth. "Jesus fuck. I've about had my fill of body-dragging for one night."

Steve clapped him on the shoulder. "No rest for the wicked, bro. Let's move."

They returned to the Cadillac. Wayne slipped in behind the wheel and Steve took the shotgun seat. He tugged the guard's gun out of his waistband and thumbed the safety to the off position.

Wayne started the car.

Steve instinctively switched on the radio and cranked the volume. "Sympathy for the Devil" by the Rolling Stones poured out of the car's high-end speakers, sounding magnificently loud and ominous.

Steve threw his head back and cackled loudly.

Wayne couldn't help it. He laughed, too. It should have felt wrong to laugh in the wake of the evening's carnage. But it didn't.

Fucking hypocrites.

Steve shouted over the music: "GUN IT!"

Wayne revved the Cadillac's engine.

Then he put the car in gear and slammed the gas pedal to the floor. The Cadillac took off like something shot from a rocket. The arm gate shattered in a spray of red-and-white splinters as the big car bulled through it and hurtled toward the building at the end of the long driveway.

Fourteen
Your Pretty Face is Going to Hell

A sensation as of rising up from murky depths. A drowning victim floating to the surface, glimpsing a diffused glimmer of light that grows rapidly brighter. Almost feels like flying, ascending to the heavens on a beam of radiant bliss.

Sybil Huffington awoke with a weak gasp. Her eyes fluttered open and the first thing she saw was the same face she'd glimpsed before losing consciousness. A slim, pretty girl with a dark wedge of hair and pale skin. Cynthia Laymon. The name came to her from the ether, delivered to her conscious mind alone, with no accompanying background information.

The girl grinned and exclaimed, "Queen Cunt lives!"

A male voice: "Shit."

Sybil frowned.

Queen Cunt?

In the normal course of events, this girl would pay dearly for such offensive insolence. A week spent in the claustrophobic darkness of an isolation room. A daily administration of corrective corporal punishment. At the SIMRC, that could mean anything from paddlings to lashings with a leather strop. Perhaps even a private, late-night disciplinary session or two in her own office. Followed, perhaps, by another hole for Quigley to dig.

But Quigley wouldn't be digging any more six-foot holes. He was dead, a walking corpse. As were the girls she'd killed. Three of the four, anyway.

Things were about as far from "normal" as she could imagine.

The girl slapped her. Hard.

And laughed.

Sybil groaned and tried to lift her head, but the effort triggered shockwaves of pain. The back of her head touched the floor again and she winced. A big spot there felt tender and moist. A flash of memory then—her feet slipping on the wet floor, the sudden plummet and the hard impact, the mammoth burst of pain, the voices, and the girl hovering over her just before she blacked out.

She blinked and looked past the girl. They were no longer in the corridor. This room had two cots, a small chest of drawers, and a closet. A dorm room, and perhaps one of the most utilitarian she'd seen. The parents of the girls residing here had elected not to pay more for extra amenities. Sybil experienced a flicker of the dark thrill she always felt upon entering such a room. Deprivation engenders a sense of hopelessness. So often she would glimpse despair in the faces girls such as this one. Which was exactly what she wanted them to feel. Their tears made her smile and shiver with delight.

This was but an echo of that feeling. It passed in an instant. Now it was her turn to know hopelessness. The fall hadn't paralyzed her, thank heaven for small blessings. She had feeling in all extremities. Could move her hands and feet. But she was immobilized nonetheless. Every attempt at movement sparked another lash of teeth-gnashing pain. Escape under own power was not possible.

She spied a man standing in a rear corner of the room. Average height and weight. About thirty. Hispanic. Maybe Mexican. He stood with his back to them, facing a window overlooking the rear of the building. The man wore the uniform of a janitor.

Another flash of memory—the yellow WET FLOOR sign.

The man's name came to her. Romero. Hector Romero.

Steeling herself against the pain, she lifted her head and raised her voice: "Hector!"

The man flinched but kept his back to her. "Yes?"

"I am injured and require immediate medical assistance." Her voice was invested with the usual steely authority. It never failed to snap her underlings into instant action. "Summon a doctor at once."

Hector didn't move. Didn't say a word.

Sybil seethed. She propped herself on an elbow, gritting her teeth against the surge of pain. "Hector! Stop standing there like a useless lump and do as I say!"

Hector continued his maddening impression of a statue. This further stoked the embers of her incipient rage, but she dismissed him for the moment, shifting her focus to the girl, who still wore that leering grin. She ached to slap it off her face. "You're Cynthia Laymon, correct?"

Cynthia sucked in a quick breath, slapped a hand to her chest. Her eyes bugged out and her jaw dropped open. An exaggerated level of mock astonishment. "Oh, Miss Huffington, I am so honored! You remembered my name! Me, little miss nothing" She shook her head and grinned broadly again. "Will wonders never cease?"

Sybil wanted to wrap her hands around the little bitch's slender throat and squeeze hard. Squeeze until her eyes bugged out for real and her pale flesh turned purple. She did a calculation of how much physical effort it would require and balanced this against the pain such an effort would cost her.

She cursed inwardly.

Not possible.

Not yet.

She bit her lip, forced herself back to a level of relative calm before speaking again. "Think about this, Miss Laymon. Your friend the mop-pusher risks only his job by disobeying me. But you, young lady, you risk a good deal more." A corner of her mouth curled some, a malignant half-smile empty of humor and loaded with dark promise. "How does a month in an isolation room sound? Just for a start, of course."

What happened next stunned her.

The girl's big grin vanished. Her eyes went dead. Her jaw quivered. She curled a hand into a fist and a moment later Sybil felt a crash of knuckles against her nose. Cartilage snapped. Blood gushed. The back of her head thumped the floor and pain burned in every nerve-ending. Then the girl was straddling her, screaming at her, her fists coming down again and again, a blur of motion as violent rage possessed her. Her face was so twisted with raw fury that she barely looked human, more like a vengeful demon in humanoid form. After a while, Sybil stopped feeling the barrage of blows. Her vision blurred and the girl was just a pale blob atop her.

Then she was gone, pulled away in mid-shriek by Hector Romero.

Cynthia flailed against the janitor for a few moments, then collapsed sobbing into his arms. Sybil's vision cleared some and she watched the brown-skin man stroke her hair and whisper soothing things into her ear. There was something between them. An emotional connection, at least. Could be they were even lovers. It made her sick, the idea of a pretty thing like Cynthia Laymon finding solace in the arms of a filthy little foreigner. She vowed to see him deported back to his shithole of origin as soon possible.

Of course, she would have to survive this insane night first.

Which was seeming less likely by the moment.

But that was no reason to just give up. The girl was distracted, lost in the swell of some ridiculous emotional storm. The time to act was now.

Sybil bit her lower lip hard, drew blood as she raised herself to an elbow again. Wave upon wave of pain coursed through her, caused hot tears to spill from her eyes, but she kept pushing herself. In a moment she was sitting upright. She glanced over her shoulder. The doors to these rooms locked from the outside, but this one was open by the slightest crack. She felt the first euphoric rush of impending triumph. She could do this. It was really possible. She just had to get to her feet.

She steeled herself against the pain one more time and began to rise . . . only to topple backward again as something hard slammed into her stomach. A foot. She'd been kicked. Then Cynthia Laymon was hovering over her again, eyes gleaming with a rage that bordered on madness, face twisted in a bitter sneer.

The girl was screaming again, raging at her, but measuring her fury just enough to render her words intelligible: "GODDAMN YOU FUCKING CUNT BITCH FROM HELL! SINCE YOU'VE GOT SUCH A GOOD FUCKING MEMORY TELL ME WHAT HAPPENED TO KATHY RUSSO! COME ON BITCH! YOU REMEMBER KATHY I FUCKING KNOW YOU DO!"

The pain was astonishing. Like a hyper-ravenous virus or parasite poisoning her blood and burning through every nerve in her body. Despite this, the name the girl invoked did register. She'd killed two SIMRC girls. Anna Kincaid, of course, and earlier in the year she'd strangled Kathy Russo with a twisted length of nylon hose. But . . . how could this stupid girl know anything about that? The cover-up had been executed with great care and precision. Officially, Russo was a runaway, and there was nothing—not one teeny iota of lingering trace evidence—to point a finger at Sybil Huffington.

Somehow, Cynthia Laymon suspected her anyway. It made her question whether she'd truly been as circumspect in her trysts with the girls as she'd imagined.

As if sensing her thoughts, Cynthia supplied the answer in a more subdued voice: "This is my second time here this year, Syphilis. Your stupid heavy metal cure didn't take the first time and my shitbag parents sent me back. Kathy was my roommate first time around. She told me about those late night counseling sessions in your office."

Sybil felt something cold slide down her gullet and slither around her heart. A whimper escaped her throat and tears began to leak from her eyes. The display of emotion had nothing to do with anything as ridiculous as remorse, of course. It was all self-pity. She didn't deserve to be in this situation. Didn't deserve to have her carefully constructed house of cards crashing down on her this way. She was better than this. A member of the social elite. The scorn this white trash trollop was directing at her was an affront against everything she believed about herself.

Something wet splashed her chin.

She swiped at the moisture.

Saliva.

The nasty little bitch spit on me!

Before she could begin entertaining more fantasies of revenge, the girl was on top of her again, straddling her midsection and leaning close, voice dropping to a fierce whisper as she said, "Girls talk, Syphilis. Don't you know that? She told me every sick little detail. The spankings. The stupid costumes. All the strange things you made her say and do. What kind of freak are you?"

Sybil's jaw quivered. She prayed for the girl to lean closer. How she'd love to take a bite out of that pretty face. The thought triggered a tingle of strange desire. She imagined chewing and swallowing the girl's flesh and felt her nipples stiffen. Strange. She thought of the bite the zombie had taken out of her and felt that same odd tingle. The wound was pulsing. Her whole arm felt raw with infection.

Cynthia leaned an inch closer.

Sybil opened her mouth, licked her lips. She saw the girl's pulse tick in her throat and squirmed beneath her. That throat . . . that beautiful throat . . . how tender it looked . . .

How . . . exquisite.

The flesh-lust began to consume her, so much so that Cynthia's next words barely registered: "Then one night Kathy went up to your office and never came back." She sneered again. "I never believed that runaway bullshit. Kathy wouldn't do that. She really wanted to please you, believe it or not. Yet for some reason she was gone forever. You killed her, didn't you, Syphilis?"

Sybil smiled. The pain was fading fast, replaced by a sensual warmth that simultaneously stimulated multiple appetites and filled her with a feeling of well-being. It was marvelous, like the way she'd once imagined it would feel to bask in God's light.

She laughed. "Yes. I killed her. It felt . . . sooooo . . . goooooooooodddd . . ."

The confession felt better than good.

Ecstatic. Yes. The feeling was so all-consuming it never occurred to her to wonder what—short of a super-sized injection of morphine—could have erased the pain so completely in so short a time. If someone had told her she was in the process of dying—and transforming—she wouldn't have been concerned. It would have seemed a price worth paying to feel this way.

Her odd behavior inflamed Cynthia's righteous rage again. "Hector! Give it to me!"

Sybil laughed at the unintentional pornographic undertone in the girl's words.

But then the girl had something in her hands and she stopped laughing. A pillow. Encased in one of the crisp white pillowcases the SIMRC's maid staff changed out every day. She frowned, not understanding what the little bitch had in mind. Then the pillow was on her face, its softness pressing hard against her, sealing off all air passages. A burst of panic penetrated the sense of euphoria and she began to thrash beneath the girl, bucking hard, her fury and energy a match for any rodeo bull fighting to dislodge a rider.

The girl slipped. The pillow slid away from her and Sybil gasped for air. One of her arms came unpinned, and before the girl could situate the pillow atop her face again, Sybil seized her by a wrist and pulled her close.

The girl screamed, this time from terror rather than rage.

Sybil snarled, opened her mouth wide, and sank her teeth into that tender, sweet flesh. The sense of euphoria returned as hot blood flowed into her mouth. The violence, coupled with the feel of the blood and raw meat on her tongue, increased the feeling tenfold.

She chewed the girl's flesh.

And moaned.

Scratch that, a thousandfold.

The girl screamed some more, but it was a more ragged sound. A dying sound. She tried to pull free, but Sybil held her tight. Pulled her close again. And buried her teeth in one of the girl's cheeks. She wrenched her head and a big flap of flesh pulled loose, exposing muscle and sinew. The girl sobbed weakly and fell against her. Then Hector was there, come to his young lover's aid at last. A little too late, alas.

She tossed the dying girl aside and jabbed fingers into the janitor's eye sockets, the digits punching through the orbs with astonishing ease. When she had finished with Hector, she tossed him aside and staggered out of the room.

By then she was no longer really Sybil Huffington.

She was something better.

Something stronger.

Something very, very hungry.

Fifteen
My Aim is True

The guard jerked away from Quigley. Blood fountained from his shoulder as he staggered to his left and fell against the other guard, who recoiled in disgust and shoved his badly injured comrade away from him—back into the outstretched arms of the reanimated maintenance man. The man had time to scream one more time before Quigley tore open his jugular vein.

The other guard stumbled backward, struck the edge of a table, and lost his balance. As he toppled to the floor, instinct caused him to hold a hand out in front of him, presumably to absorb the brunt of the impact. But the hand landed at a bad angle and took the free-falling guard's full weight. There was a sound like the snapping of a branch, then a wail of agony. The sharp angle of the break caused a shard of splintered bone to pierce the man's flesh. Zombie Whore 1 fell upon him and buried her teeth in the side of his neck. The guard shrieked again and his body spasmed. He made a last-ditch effort to dislodge the zombie as he got his good hand beneath him and pushed himself to his knees. But the zombie held tight and tore loose a hunk of bloody flesh. The guard wobbled and the zombie bore him back to the floor. He was finished moments later.

Melissa observed the display of total incompetency from a prone position several feet away. The bullet had winged her shoulder. She'd lucked out. Although it stung like a bastard, the wound was minor. A graze, nothing more. But luck would only get her so far. She needed to get off her ass—pronto—and run like hell.

Lindy screamed again.

Get up and help her, you fucking idiot!

Melissa braced her hands against the floor and started to push herself up.

Then David was standing over her, his good-looking, faintly effeminate features awash in blood and flecks of meat. His mouth opened wide and he bared his teeth at her. A sound like the low warning growl of a guard dog rumbled out of him, followed by an altogether different sound that might have been funny under drastically different circumstances—a very loud, and very protracted, burp.

More of a belch, really.

Zombie Belushi.

Starring in Animal Living Dead House.

She drew her legs back and kicked out at David's kneecaps. He flew backward and struck a reanimated guard. The guard stumbled backward several steps but managed to remain upright, while David landed in an awkward heap on the floor. Melissa got her feet beneath her and levered herself upright. She scanned the floor for the knife, but spied something better—a nickel-plated automatic, its barrel wedged in the narrow crack between two snack machines. She hurried across the room, sliding for a moment in a slick of blood, and knelt to retrieve the discarded weapon. She pulled it free and whirled about in time to fire a shot at the guard who'd only moments earlier used the same gun to wound her. He was a zombie now. The bullet punched a hole through his belly and knocked him back a step. She raised the gun's barrel to aim the next shot at his head.

Then she heard Lindy wail and turned in that direction instead, her finger frozen on the trigger. Lindy had her hands splayed flat against Anna Kincaid's busty chest. Her head was turned away from the zombie, one cheek pressed against the brick wall. The zombie's lips stretched wide as it extended its teeth toward Lindy's scrawny neck. The last of Lindy's strength ebbed as Melissa watched. The battle was lost. Sensing this, the zombie reared its head back, preparing to strike.

Melissa scampered across the floor again, knocking over a chair and sliding for another precarious moment in the blood slick before arriving at the last possible moment to jam the automatic's barrel against the zombie's temple. She jerked the trigger and experienced an instant of primal satisfaction as its head blew apart. But her breath caught in her throat as she saw she'd been too late after all. At some point in all the confusion the zombie had managed to partially disembowel the spunky young girl. A loop of intestine hung out of a bloody rent in her flesh. Melissa sobbed as she watched Lindy's eyes go blank. Lindy's body began a slow, horrible slide toward the floor—and then stopped. Her chin lifted from her chest as a new kind of pseudo-life dawned in those glassy eyes.

So it's just me now, Melissa thought. *Alone in a room full of zombies.*

This is so fucked.

At what point had her life turned into some sleazy late night cable movie?

Lindy's mouth opened and emitted that graveyard hiss she'd heard issuing from the other zombies. The dead girl pushed herself away from the wall and took a tentative step in Melissa's direction. Then another, longer stride, but this time she slipped in a pool of her own blood and viscera and crashed to the floor. The misstep didn't faze the newborn zombie. It rolled over and began to crawl toward Melissa, one hand extended toward her ankle.

Melissa sighed.

"Goddamn."

She aimed the gun at the back of Lindy's head, averted her gaze, and pulled the trigger. She didn't see the girl's head erupt in a spray of blood, bone fragments, and brain matter, but she knew her aim had been on the money. Otherwise that grasping hand would have seized her ankle by now. Would, perhaps, have yanked her to the floor.

Then it would have been all over.

And given the hopeless, empty feeling consuming her, maybe that would have been for the best.

She turned away from the dead girl and faced the remaining zombies, who were converging on her from seemingly every direction now, eight arms reaching for her, four stupid eating machines intent on devouring her warm flesh. She stepped backward over Lindy's corpse, retreating into the same corner where the girl had made her ill-fated last stand against Anna Kincaid. She glanced at the shiny gun clenched in her fist as she tried to quickly assess her situation.

Basic fact number one—she didn't know shit about guns.

Other than point, squeeze, BANG!

She didn't know how many bullets a full magazine would contain, much less how many remained. It was just possible she might have enough time left to take careful aim at each undead motherfucker's head and pull the trigger. But would there be enough bullets?

Moreover, would there be one left for her if things went wrong?

Only one way to find out.

She aimed the gun at Zombie Whore 1's forehead, extending her arm and bracing the butt of the gun with the palm of her left hand in imitation of a shooting stance she'd seen actors use on shows like Miami Vice. Maybe it was the right way to do it and maybe it wasn't. Did it really matter at this point?

She drew in a breath and held it.

Then she squeezed the trigger and the gun jumped an inch or so as the bullet discharged. The round buzzed over the top of Zombie Whore 1's head, but failed to even nick her scalp.

Lesson number one—blowing away zombies was easier up close and personal.

"Fuck it."

She stepped out of the corner and took aim at the dead hooker again, this time training the gun's sight dead-center on the thing's blood-specked face. She squeezed the trigger again and this time the bullet slammed through the bridge of the dead woman's nose. The zombie hit the floor and this time the dead bitch didn't get back up. Adrenaline kicked Melissa into a higher gear.

She thought, *GET IT DONE.*

She turned slightly and took another quick step to her left to aim the gun at the next-nearest zombie.

Too late, she felt her feet slide through the blood slick again.

This time, though, her luck ran out and she crashed to the floor. Again. Her and this fucking floor, man, they were getting intimately acquainted.

She turned onto her back with a groan and saw two zombies looming over her.

Reaching for her.

The gun was gone, lost in the fall.

She thought, *THIS IS IT.*

Then she heard new voices in the hallway. Frantic voices. Her eyes went wide as she recognized the achingly familiar timbre of one of them.

A zombie guard dropped to a knee beside her and reached for her throat.

She opened her mouth wide and screamed a single word: "*Wayne!*"

Sixteen
Break on Through

The employee entrance door at the back of the building was standing open when Wayne steered Mark Cheney's Cadillac into the small rear parking lot. Strange, given the lateness of the hour and the adverse weather conditions, but Wayne was too buoyed by this unexpected bit of good fortune to find anything about the situation alarming.

Steve threw his door open before Wayne had brought the Cadillac to a complete stop. "Let's rock and roll!"

Then he was gone, out the door and dashing across the parking lot before Wayne could reply.

"Jesus."

Steve's words echoed in his mind: *Let's rock and roll.*

Yeah, okay. Appropriate words, given the locale.

Wayne got out of the car and hurried after his friend, leaving the keys in the ignition and the engine running. The better to effect a rapid retreat on the way out. He hoped.

Steve came to an abrupt halt just outside the door, but before Wayne could wonder about that his gaze was drawn to a distant wedge of light at the far end of the building.

Holy shit, he thought. *Another open door.*

Okay, so the SIMRC was no maximum security kennel for hardcase murderers and rapists. It wasn't San fucking Quentin. But it wasn't summer camp either. He recalled the murderous guard's vague account of a disturbance in the building and felt his stomach clench with fear again.

He was within ten feet of Steve now, his gaze still on the other open door.

Dude, this is fuckin' strange. It's like open house night at—"

Then he was next to Steve and saw what had stopped his friend in his tracks. Bile filled his throat, too much to choke back this time. His cheeks puffed wide, then he bent forward and projectile-vomited the remains of his Wendy's dinner, splattering puke all over the top of the cannibal girl's head.

"Dude, gross."

Wayne gagged again and clapped a hand on his friend's shoulder to stave off a collapse.

"What the fuck, man?" He swallowed hard. "The hell's wrong with her?"

Steve shrugged. "Kinda looks like a . . . zombie."

"Bullshit."

But this was said automatically, a rote, rational world knee-jerk response. Steve didn't bother to refute it. There was the evidence of their eyes and that was enough. The girl was a zombie. No doubt about it. Not a cannibal, as he'd first thought. Nope, she was a walking, flesh-eating corpse. And she was clad in a perved-out porn movie version of a Catholic school girl outfit. A very short pleated skirt and a tight white blouse tied off at the midriff. Blond hair in pigtails. Would have been damned sexy on any halfway attractive chick not freshly risen from the goddamn grave. But there was nothing sexy about this creature. Its body was dessicated, once-white flesh turned dark with rot and crawling with maggots where it still clung to bone. More maggots writhed in the thing's eye sockets. The creature was bent over the body of a guard, gnarled hands buried deep in the dead man's ripped-open belly. The guard's body was propping open the door. The zombie lifted its face from a mound of guts and looked up at them. Vomit streamed over taut features. It opened its mouth and a withered wedge of blackened tongue slithered out to lick at the bile.

Steve put a hand to his mouth. "Aw, shit."

The dead girl's face received another vomit bath a moment later It didn't seem to mind.

89

What was left of Kathy Russo, the last of Sybil Huffington's victims to claw its way out of the ground, even seemed to enjoy it in some dim way.

Steve cast a sideways glance at Wayne. "Do me one favor, bro?"

Wayne stared at the dead girl, grimacing as she stuffed a sausage-like length of intestine between her cracked and blackened lips. "Ugh . . . what, man?"

Steve made a sound of disgust and wiped his mouth with the back of a hand. "Years from now, when we're telling stories about this shit, what say we leave out the bit about the puking?"

"Why?"

"Makes us sound like a couple of pussies."

Wayne nodded. "Okay."

Steve pointed the gun he'd commandeered at the zombie's head and pulled the trigger. The bullet blew the zombie's moldering face apart and sent its body flying back through the open door, landing in a sprawl in the short strip of hallway beyond.

Wayne looked askance at him. "Why'd you do that?"

Steve's grunted. "Dude, that's what you do with zombies—shoot 'em in the head. You've seen the movies."

Wayne's first impulse was to point out the obvious, that zombie movies were a bunch of made-up bullshit. And that when confronted with a walking, flesh-eating corpse in real life, you shouldn't look to some cinematic pile of garbage for helpful hints on how to deal with them. But there was no arguing with results. The zombie was dead. Dead again. Double dead. Whatever. It was as still as a mannequin and showed no signs of getting up again. And shooting it couldn't be called an act of murder. You couldn't murder a thing that was already dead.

"Okay, zombies. They're real, I guess. But in the movies, there's always some vague cause for the undead uprising. Toxic waste spill. Voodoo. Some kinda shit like that."

Steve nodded. "Right. Or my favorite, radiation from a comet."

They looked at each other, eyes going wide.

"Dude."

"That fuckin' meteor."

"Yeah."

Wayne dropped to his knees and began to fumble with the dead guard's belt.

"What are you doing?"

He found the dead man's gun, slipped it out of its holster.

"Oh. Good thinking."

Wayne stood up and returned his father's unloaded .45 to his jacket pocket. Maybe more zombies were waiting for them inside. Maybe not. Either way, he meant to be ready. The unloaded gun bluff had been a good idea in theory, but things had changed.

Steve stepped past the guard's corpse and entered the building Wayne started to follow him inside, but felt something snag his pants leg. He glanced down and saw the disemboweled guard looking up at him, eyes open and staring, some kind of awareness there. And something else. A need. Hunger, maybe. Fuck. The dead man's hand slid up the back of his leg in a disturbing parody of a lover's caress. Wayne flinched, but kept his cool, aimed the gun at the thing's face.

A calm, slow squeeze of the trigger.

A flat but solid bang, a jolt that traveled the length of his arm and jarred his shoulder, and the guard flopped back to the ground, his existence as a reanimated corpse mercifully contained to a handful of seconds. Wayne stared at the sickening physical damage wrought by the bullet for a long moment. Then he felt Steve's hand on his shoulder, turning him away from the grisly tableau. They moved past a deserted guard station and arrived at another door. This one was closed, but there was a small, wire-lined window set in its center. They took turns peeking through it. What they saw was a long, bland strip of hallway that appeared to extend all the way to the far end of the building. All the way, Wayne realized, to the approximate location of that other open door.

As Wayne watched, two men abruptly came barreling around the corner at the far end of the hallway, heads down and legs pumping, running flat-out, as if the hounds of hell were nipping at their heels. Which could only mean one thing. More zombies. More danger. The impression of a situation spiraling out of control became more firmly entrenched in Wayne's mind. The men were SIMRC guards. One short and dumpy, the other lean and not as short. Somehow the short, fat one was outdistancing the better conditioned man, perhaps propelled forward by one mega-mother of an adrenaline blast. As the men drew nearer, terror was evident in their expressions.

Steve looked at Wayne. "Those guys are coming through this door in about ten seconds."

Wayne nodded. "Yeah."

He stepped back from the door and raised his gun to shoulder level. Steve did the same, stepping back several paces in the other direction. Wayne stared at the door and tried not to listen to the hammering of his heart. Sweat beaded on his brow and his knees shook.

He drew in a breath, willed himself to be calm.

The door slammed inward and the two men piled into the room. Their eyes went wide when they saw the guns leveled at them. They screeched to a halt, breathing hard. One man instinctively dropped a hand to his holster.

Steve's face screwed up as he barked a command: "FREEZE!"

The guard's hand was still in motion, undoing the holster strap, fingers curling around the butt of the gun. A shot rang out, sharp like a firecracker report in the enclosed room. Only way louder. Blood bloomed from a hole in the man's left shoulder. He cried out and fell back through the open door. Wayne saw the other man go for his gun and stepped forward, rapping the butt of his gun against the man's nose. Cartilage snapped and blood rushed from his nostrils. The man dropped to his knees, wailing and blubbering like a baby. Wayne raised the gun again and delivered a knockout blow. He looked through the door and saw Steve kneeling over the man in the hallway, securing him with handcuffs. Wayne dropped to his knees and did the same with the man he'd knocked out.

Some distant part of him was appalled by his participation in these violent acts. But on another, more pragmatic level he recognized he was merely doing what was necessary. What was expedient. These were the civilized elements of his psyche weighing in on the situation. Another part of him, one not even all that distant, derived a primitive kind of exhilaration from it all. He was still shaking some, but he felt good, energized. Ready to fight some more.

Which was good, because it was looking like there was a lot of fighting left to be done.

A dim but high-pitched sound emanated from the far end of the hallway.

A scream?

He was on his feet and moving before he could even think about what he was doing. The sound came again and his legs began to move faster. Steve jumped up and hurried after him. That high-pitched noise came yet again, louder and shriller this time. Screams. Definitely screams.

"Dude. Fuck," Steve said between pants as they began to run. "This shit has true bloodbath potential written all over it. You know that?"

Wayne didn't answer. He knew it, all right. They were nearing a junction where the hallway dead-ended and turned to the right. They rounded the corner and the sounds of struggle grew suddenly louder.

Steve pointed to an open archway up ahead a bit on their left. "That way. In there."

Then a voice he knew boomed out: "Wayne!"

Melissa!

He dashed through the archway and saw bodies dead on the floor. Some fresh, some showing evidence of graveyard decay. Blood was everywhere. Skull fragments, brain matter, and loops of intestine. Zombies crowded around another body on the floor, this one still alive, struggling and thrashing against them. The person on the floor screamed and Wayne knew at once it was Melissa. Still alive, but not for much longer if he didn't do something. Gritting his teeth, he stepped up behind one of the zombies, aimed the gun at the back of its head, and squeezed the trigger. The executed zombie toppled forward, landing atop the struggling girl and causing a zombie on the opposite side of her to fall backward.

Wayne and Steve went to work, dispatching the remaining flesh-eaters with quick efficiency. Then Wayne hauled the first one off of Melissa, helped her to her feet, and drew her into his arms. She fell against him and sobbed against his neck for several long moments. He stroked her hair and made mindless cooing noises in her ear. He looked over her shoulder at Steve, who was standing at the archway, watching them with grim-faced solemnity. He glanced out at the hallway, then looked at Wayne again and pointed at his wrist, telling him they didn't have time for this. Wayne mouthed the words 'I know' and began to gently disengage himself from Melissa. She clung to him fiercely for a moment, then relented, staring up at him with eyes brimming with tears.

"Oh Wayne . . . it was . . . horrible . . ."

Wayne glanced around the room again, taking in the carnage, allowing himself a moment to absorb the horror that had occurred here. His heart ached at the knowledge of what Melissa must have gone through, the desperation she must have known during her fight to survive. For the first time Wayne knew with absolute certainty he had done the right thing by coming to this place tonight. Had he allowed common sense to trump gut instinct, he would be at home right now, maybe eating some popcorn and watching a late-night horror movie. Talk about bitter irony.

And Melissa would be dead. No doubt about it. End of fucking story.

But she wasn't dead. And he was with her again, at long last.

Something like triumph began to well up inside him.

He put a hand to her cheek and forced a smile. "It's okay now. You're okay. And we're getting out of this fucking place right now."

He began to steer her toward the archway, but she twisted away from him. "We can't leave. Not yet."

Wayne frowned. "What? Why?"

She made an exasperated sound and waved her arm in the direction of the archway. Wayne guessed the gesture was meant to encompass the entire building. "I want to burn this place to the ground."

Steve came back into the room. "Whoa. You serious?"

Her nod was emphatic. Her eyes stayed on Wayne. They still glimmered with moisture, but a fierce determination burned beneath. "I'm serious. But first we get all the other kids out of here. This place is *evil*, Wayne. At first I just wanted out. One of the so-called teachers raped me in his office."

Wayne's breath caught in his throat. Emotions warred within him. Grief over what she must have felt while it was happening, the pure horror of the experience, and for what it must have cost her emotionally in the aftermath. And an incipient murderous rage. "Who did it? Tell me his name."

"His name's not important right now." She swiped fresh tears from her eyes with an impatient gesture. "He did it and that's why I called you. I just wanted out. But now . . . after all this . . ." She indicated the recent struggle with a sweep of her hand. "I can't leave my friends here. I told you, this place is evil. It has to burn."

"Okay. Shit." Wayne ran a hand through his hair and began to pace the room, taking care to step around all the sprawled bodies as he thought about it. "We might even have time to do it. The guards are all out of the picture, far as I can tell. But how do we get everybody out? Aren't they all locked up?"

A small, fragile smile tinged the corners of Melissa's mouth. "Easy."

She knelt next to one of the dead guards, snagged a ring of keys from his belt, and stood again. "There's a key on here just like the one my friend David used to get me out of my room tonight." Her fragile smile broke apart, gave way to an expression fraught with grief. "David died tonight." She pointed to a body on the floor. "He put his ass on the line for me and now he's gone. It's my fault."

Wayne frowned. "Melissa, no. You can't blame—"

"It's my fault," she reiterated, voice louder this time, invested with powerful, undeniable emotion. "That's the truth and that's that. But we're past that now. I'm not gonna let anybody else get hurt by this place. Not if I can help it."

Wayne considered pointing out that the SIMRC hadn't killed her friend. Zombies had done that. But he saw the steely resolve in her eyes and decided against it. Besides, she had a point. This place really was evil. Its sole function was to purge every non-conformist instinct from the psyches of rebellious children. To snuff even the slightest spark of individuality or creativity. To turn them into mindless, well-behaved automatons. A different kind of zombie.

So fuck it.

He smiled. "Okay."

Melissa returned the smile and moved close to him. "I love you."

Then she kissed him, throwing herself into it, her passion igniting his own. She felt so perfect against him. His senses tingled and every nerve-ending seemed to explode with sensation. He grew hard as she pressed against him. Then she broke the embrace and grinned at him.

Wayne caught his breath and said, "Holy shit. I love you, too."

Steve coughed. "A-hem. Okay, lovebirds. If we're gonna torch this place and liberate the inmates, we best get to work. So let's stop fucking around." He winked at Wayne as he knelt to retrieve the other fallen guard's keys. "There'll be time for that later."

Wayne sighed. "Yeah. Okay. So where do we go?"

Melissa moved through the archway into the hallway. "This way."

Wayne and Steve followed her out of the gore-soaked break room. Out in the hallway, they turned left and followed her a short distance to a closed door.

Melissa paused with her hand on the doorknob. "The dorm rooms are all on the second floor. It shouldn't take long to get everybody out."

Wayne nodded. "Okay. Cool."

Melissa turned the knob and pulled the door open.

Steve said, "Wait. I heard—"

A zombie appeared from seemingly nowhere. A Hispanic man in a janitor's uniform.

t seized Melissa by the neck and pulled her through the opening.

Seventeen
Fresh Flesh

The thing that had been Sybil Huffington was not like the other zombies. The others were just eating machines on legs. Stupid monsters inhabiting bodies vacated by human souls. Sybil shared their hunger for warm human flesh. But the black, diseased thing that passed for her soul remained tied to its physical shell. Though zombified, she still had a vague conception of herself as a personality, as Sybil Marie Huffington, a respected woman in some position of authority. And she had retained a level of cognitive function. Her brain continued to process actual thoughts and ideas, and she possessed a basic ability to verbalize these things through rudimentary English. She was thus able to exercise a degree of cunning.

Watching from the second floor landing, she smiled as the dead janitor attacked the living things below. The screams of the female were especially pleasing to her ears. Three more zombies descended the stairs and waded into the melee. These were new recruits, kids she'd killed after entering their rooms with a passkey. She'd hoped to send a whole army of zombies against the living things, but she'd known there wouldn't be enough time to create one. Instead, she'd guided this small contingent to the staircase, hoping they would deter her adversaries long enough to build a more formidable force.

Sybil's smile broadened as she watched one of her minions take a big bite out of a living thing's forearm. The high spurt of blood was a beautiful thing to behold. She longed to fill her mouth with it. The urge was so powerful she even took a tentative step toward the staircase. But a scream from the second floor hallway shifted her attention. She turned and glimpsed the first girl she'd transformed—

the one who'd tried to smother her—and smiled again. The girl had extracted another of the living things from its room and had pinned it to the floor. The living girl screamed and thrashed against her zombie assailant, but failed to dislodge her. The girl pinned to the floor was particularly nubile, with lush curves and big breasts that strained against a tangled pajama top, and she had a mass of blonde hair as radiant as the sun's rays.

Sybil lurched through the door and staggered down the hallway, dropping to her knees beside the struggling girls. The living girl's eyes locked on her for a moment, her breath catching in her throat as recognition dawned. Then she realized the SIMRC's headmistress was also a zombie and loosed a shrill scream. Sybil tried to scream back at her, but all that emerged from her throat was a dry exhalation of rancid breath. The girl screamed again as the zombie girl atop her bit off her thumb. A high spray of dark blood arced out of the mangled stump. Some of it splashed Sybil's face, entering her open, leering mouth, the taste of it exquisite on her tongue.

She ripped at the living girl's pajama top. Fabric tore and plastic buttons popped into the air. And now the girl's large, jiggling breasts were on display. The sight of them inflamed Sybil. She shoved the zombie girl away and fell atop the nubile blonde. The girl tried to get up, but Sybil was able to keep her pinned to the floor. She bared her teeth at the girl and hissed like a snake. The girl screamed again, but this time the sound trailed away to a mewling blubber.

Sybil latched onto one of the exposed breasts, drawing the large nipple deep into her mouth. She lapped at the nipple with her rough tongue, eliciting more squeals of pain. But soon the flesh-eating imperative inherent in her new nature overrode the echo of carnal lust and she bit into the breast, felt blood fill her mouth for a moment. Then she wrenched her head as hard as she could and tore loose a hunk of flesh. It felt so good sliding down her gullet that she immediately took another bite.

Then another.

The girl's struggles weakened, then finally she surrendered to the inevitable. In mere moments she was one of them, a new soldier in the war against living things.

Sybil rose and licked delicious blood from her lips.

Then she found the passkey again and lurched toward the nearest closed door.

Eighteen
Crash Course in
Brain Surgery

Steve leaped through the open door an instant before Wayne, slamming into Melissa and the zombie at knee-level, a devastating tackle that would have been the envy of any NFL cornerback. The three crashed into a mop cart. The cart spun toward Wayne as they fell in a heap to the floor. Wayne kicked the cart away and was moving to assist Steve and Melissa when he saw the other zombies descending the staircase. They were teenagers, likely no older than he was. But their hungry, vacant expressions provided sufficient evidence of zombie transformation.

Watching the carnage from the second floor landing was another zombie. This one was older. Someone formerly in a position of authority at the SIMRC, he guessed. Her clothes were in tatters and covered in blood. Her face was flecked with blood. None of this bothered him half as much as the strange smile pulling at the edges of her mouth.

A smiling zombie?

Something about it just seemed . . . wrong.

A high-pitched scream from the floor jolted him. He tore his gaze from the strange zombie and saw something that nearly made his heart seize. The zombie janitor had gotten his mouth on one of Steve's arms. The slavering creature growled and bit off a chunk of flesh. Wayne kicked the zombie under the chin with all the force he could muster and it went sailing backward. Melissa scrambled to her feet and moved away as Wayne stepped up to the zombie and pointed his gun at its forehead. He squeezed the trigger. A hole appeared in the zombie's forehead and blood splashed the wall behind it.

Wayne stood there shaking for a moment, struggling to maintain control as he watched the dead thing hit the wall and slide slowly to its knees.

Melissa let out a shriek. "Wayne!"

She pointed to something beyond him. He turned and saw that the zombie kids had reached the bottom of the staircase. He gave himself the mental equivalent of a slap—*get your shit together!* — and moved to place himself between his friends and the approaching threat. He raised his gun, trained the sight on the forehead of the nearest one, and paused for a moment as his gaze flicked upward. The strange lady zombie was gone. He had a feeling he'd have to deal with her soon. And though he couldn't have said why, the prospect of a confrontation with her unsettled him more than any of the many other horrific things that had happened thus far.

He shook his head, again forced himself to focus.

The lead zombie, a boy of about sixteen with a mop of curly brown hair, was within six feet of him. Wayne perfected his aim and squeezed the trigger. The bullet hit the boy in the cheek and sent him stumbling backward. The zombie bounced off one of its comrades and staggered forward again, arms reaching for Wayne.

Wayne cursed.

The brain, dumbass.

You have to blow its fucking brains out.

Wayne aimed again, squeezed the trigger again, and this time the bullet penetrated forehead and voided brainpan as it exited the back of the dead boy's head. Wayne put down the remaining two zombies more efficiently—one bullet each to the head. He looked at the sprawled bodies on the floor and felt a great sadness. They had all been young, of course, but they looked even younger in death. Then anger replaced sadness as an impression of innocence betrayed resonated. Anger not just at whatever force had created this zombie nightmare, but at the shortsighted stupidity and ignorance of the parents who had sent their children to this wretched place.

Wayne turned to look at his friends. "I'm gonna finish this. You guys stay here."

Steve's features were taut with pain. He leaned against Melissa for support, standing bare-chested, his wiry torso gleaming with sweat and blood. His denim jacket was on the floor, his Motorhead t-shirt wrapped tight around the wound on his arm. His eyes radiated defiance. "No way, bro. I'm in this with you to the end." He managed a strained smile. "Besides, I'm gonna need you around to finish me off once I start to turn."

Something fluttered inside Wayne. His brow creased in a deep frown. "What do you mean?"

Steve's laugh was a weak thing, the kind of sound a dying animal might make. "Fuck, you know. I've been *bitten*. I'm gonna turn into one of those fucking things."

"Bullshit."

"Serious, bro." He disengaged himself from Melissa and took a staggering step toward Wayne. "So far everything's been just like in the movies. I've got the zombie virus or whatever in me. It's gonna spread and I'm gonna turn. I know it and you know it, so do me a favor and stop acting like it ain't gonna happen."

Tears welled in Wayne's eyes. The prospect of losing the best friend he'd ever had made him feel empty. Hopeless. Then he looked into Steve's eyes and accepted that there was only one honorable way to go here.

He nodded. "All right. When it happens...I'll do what I have to do."

Steve clapped a hand on his shoulder. "Cool. Now let's kick some zombie ass."

The three of them stepped around the pile of bodies and headed up the staircase.

Nineteen
Stone Dead Forever

The second floor hallway was awash in blood. Pools of it on the slick floor tiles. Big splashes of grue on the walls. A number of doors stood open. Kids in their sleeping clothes—pajamas, boxers and t-shirts, or sweats and tees—battled creatures intent on devouring them. Creatures that looked like them. Young and pajama-clad. Former friends and fellow sufferers, transformed into monsters driven only by simple, deadly instinct.

But maybe not so simple. One among them, at least, retained some level of human-like intellect, enough to know how to get the rooms open in order to extract fresh meat. He glimpsed the older female emerging from one of the doors with a young girl in tow. Of course. The smiling zombie. She dragged the girl by her long auburn hair. The girl screamed and flailed to no effect. The zombie held her at arm's length, watching the girl struggle with a strange leer suggesting a level of perverse enjoyment not evinced by the other zombies. The auburn-haired girl's roommate followed them out of the room. She loosed a war cry of sorts and took a swing at the female zombie's head with a thick black book. A bible, maybe. The book bounced off the zombie's head. The zombie's free hand shot out, the heel of its palm connecting with the forehead of its assailant. The girl staggered backward and fell hard to the floor, the back of her head bouncing off the tiles. She didn't get back up and her roommate was left to fend for herself.

All of this was occurring beyond the larger struggle in the middle of the hallway. Again Wayne was certain this was evidence of cunning on the part of the older zombie. She was erecting a barrier between herself and the only remaining human threat. Wayne counted five other zombies and an equal number of kids struggling against them. A sudden high spurt of arterial blood signaled an abrupt tipping of the scales in favor of the zombies. Another kid dropped to the floor under the weight of two zombies.

Wayne drew a bead on the back of the nearest zombie's head. He squeezed the trigger and the high caliber bullet penetrated the crown of the boy's skull. Blood leaped from a massive forehead exit wound. Another zombie, drawn by the scent of fresh meat and the gun's report, released a girl in sweats and a SIMRC t-shirt and staggered in their direction. The girl scuttled across blood-slick tiles and disappeared through one of the open doors, kicking it shut behind her. Steve moved into position next to Wayne and fired a bullet into the approaching zombie's forehead. The zombie staggered backward, stumbling into two zombies hunched over a fallen boy on the floor. It toppled onto the back of one of the feasting zombies, which reared up, propelling the zombie carcass back toward Wayne and Steve.

Steve had time to say, "Jesus fuck."

The dead zombie plowed into him and drove him to the floor, eliciting a shriek from Melissa who knelt to drag the dead thing off of him. Another zombie lurched toward Wayne, swiping at the side of his face with an outstretched hand. One jagged fingernail etched a shallow groove in his cheek before he could shove the thing away. When it tried to rise again, he stepped on its chest and slammed it back to the floor. He pointed the gun at its face and pulled the trigger. The creature's grasping, reaching arms flopped down. Wayne stared at the thing's mangled ruin of a face. Looking at it made him think of the Billy Idol song "Eyes Without A Face." There was a better song by the same name by a punk band called The Flesheaters. He knew it from the *Return of the Living Dead* soundtrack.

"Damn." Still staring at the unmoving zombie, addressing no one but himself. "Eyes without a fuckin' face. This is so fucked up."

"What're you babbling about, bro?"

Steve was back on his feet, leaning on Melissa for support again.

This time he appeared to need the assistance more. He looked pale and his face glimmered with sweat. The shirt wrapped around his wounded forearm was soggy with blood. Wayne thought back to what Steve had said about infection. About how anyone bitten by a zombie was doomed. But was that really true? There was no way to really know, at least not until they actually saw it happen. If there was even the merest ghost of a chance of Steve surviving this, shouldn't their focus be on getting him to a hospital?

Before he could think about it any further, the zombies on the floor began to stand up. The girl they had been eating began to rise too, half-devoured organs and bits of intestine spilling out of her open stomach cavity as she got to her knees.

Great, Wayne thought. *Another fucking zombie. If we don't nip this living dead bullshit in the bud now, we'll ALL be fucking zombies.*

He shot the nearest zombie in the forehead and it dropped at once, a puppet with its strings cut. He turned and shot another zombie in the face. He heard the report of another gun next to him and saw yet another zombie fall. Steve was standing next to him, good arm extended to aim his gun. He was operating under his own power now, having rallied yet again, but Wayne had to wonder how much fight his friend had left in him.

Steve swayed on his feet.

Not much. Fuck.

The disemboweled zombie girl crawled toward them on her hands and knees, cute little pixie face lifted toward them. She had fair hair and freckles. Couldn't have been any more than sixteen. The kind of girl Wayne might have had a crush on before meeting Melissa. But there was an obscene hunger in her eyes, something utterly unrelated to whatever this girl had been prior to her death. Wayne winced as a bullet from Steve's gun blew her head apart.

Steve grimaced. "It's like we're at a zombie shooting range."

"Or a booth at a carnival," Melissa said, stepping between them. "Shoot all the zombies and win a big cuddly bear for your best girl."

Wayne nodded. "Big bucket of brains and blood, in this case."

The only zombie still mobile in the hallway was the older female. It was still toying with the auburn-haired girl Wayne had seen it drag from a room moments ago. The girl was flat on her stomach, the zombie writhing atop her, its hands clutching at her in a clearly sexual way.

Wayne's scowled. "That freaky-ass zombie bitch is pissing me off."

He began to move toward her, taking care to avoid bodies and slippery pools of blood. Steve and Melissa followed him. The zombie was too absorbed in the subjugation of its latest victim to sense their approach. It slurped at the girl's slender neck without puncturing flesh with its teeth. It slid a hand under the girl's belly, angled downward and reached for her pussy. The girl whimpered and tried to roll the zombie off her, but the creature was too strong. It slammed her back to the floor and made a sound somewhere between a dry cough and a laugh. Then it tore open the girl's flimsy top and nipped at a narrow shoulder.

Wayne shook his head. "A lesbian zombie. Okay. None of this is real. Right? I'm on some bad acid and I think I'm really in some trashy video I rented."

Steve smirked. "You don't do acid, bro. That's my thing. You never want any."

"Oh. Right. Well . . ."

Melissa sighed. "We've got to get the bitch off her."

She pushed past them and knelt over the zombie. She grabbed a fistful of the thing's blonde hair and yanked up. The creature swiped a hand at Melissa. Melissa dodged blood-caked fingernails and surged to a standing position, dragging the suddenly thrashing zombie away from the girl, who immediately scrambled out of the way.

The zombie shifted its attention fully to Melissa, delivering an open-handed blow that landed with a solid thud at such close range, its knuckles crashing into her cheek. Melissa surrendered her grip on the thing's hair and staggered back against the wall. The zombie snarled and lurched after her. Melissa raised her own gun and pulled the trigger. But she was dazed and her aim was off. The bullet hit the concrete wall and Wayne flinched away from the ricochet. Melissa immediately fired again and the next bullet shattered one of the creature's kneecaps, sending it in an awkward heap to the floor.

The girl Melissa had rescued yelped and scooted backward. "Shoot it again!" she screamed at them. "Oh, Jesus, it's still alive! Please kill it!"

One of the zombie's hands reached toward the sound of her voice.

Wayne kicked the zombie and it flopped onto its back. He pinned it to the floor by stepping on its chest. It bared its teeth and hissed at him. A shudder rippled through him as he stared into its gleaming eyes. The glassy dullness typical of the other zombies was missing. There was more to this creature than a simple need to devour flesh. Something more than primitive lust. He was sure it was consciously thinking about its situation, searching for a way to continue its struggle.

A way to escape.

A strong hand gripped his ankle.

Wayne aimed his gun at the zombie's face.

Melissa and Steve moved into position on either side of him, each also aiming their guns at the creature's leering, blood-soaked visage.

Melissa said, "This is Sybil Huffington. She runs this place. And she's an evil bitch."

Steve said, "So let's send her to hell."

Wayne's answer to this was a squeeze of his trigger.

And then another squeeze.

The other guns erupted.

The roar of gunfire filled the hallway as the three of them emptied their weapons into Sybil's head. There was precious little of it left by the time Melissa's gun clicked empty. They stood there for several long, stunned moments, the echo of the gunfire reverberating in their ears.

Then Steve's gun slipped from his fingers and landed with a clatter on the floor.

A moment later, his eyes rolled back in their sockets and he swooned.

Wayne caught the unconscious boy in his arms.

Twenty
Burn the Flames

They were back in Wayne's Jeep Cherokee now, parked across the street from the main SIMRC building. Wayne watched the orange glow visible through many of the building's windows. Somewhere shy of a hundred kids milled about on the front lawn, watching the hated building go up in flames. Some of them were dancing in the rain, which had begun to pick up a little. A celebration of sorts. To Wayne the celebrants looked vaguely like participants in some pagan ritual. Which seemed fitting, given the fundamentalist, pagan-hating principles upon which the center had been founded.

Maybe forty minutes had passed since the end of the hallway battle. Most of the intervening time had been consumed with the logistics of evacuating the building before setting it aflame. The actual act of torching the place turned out to be the easy part. A supply shed out back yielded several containers of gasoline and oil. Flammable materials in several strategic areas of the building were soaked and lit with matches and cigarette lighters.

The flames burned brighter as they watched. A window on the third floor—where the re-education classes were held—exploded outward in a spray of glass and wood splinters. Tendrils of flame licked at the outside of the building. Wayne felt a strange kind of pride as he watched the fire spread and consume the building. They had done a good job. Even the resurgent rain wouldn't save the SIMRC.

Steve's eyes fluttered as he spoke from the shotgun seat. "It's . . . beautiful." There was an aching wonderment in his slurred voice that made Wayne want to scream. "My god . . . isn't it?"

Melissa piped up from the back seat. "Yeah, Steve. It's beautiful." Her voice cracked on the last word.

Wayne knew how close to tears she was, because he felt the same way. His friend was dying. He wouldn't live even if they took him to a hospital. The infection was spreading fast. Steve already smelled like death and large patches of his skin had turned a livid shade of purple. He didn't have much time left.

Steve coughed, then managed a weak laugh. "It was worth it. Don't you fuckers ever . . . ever . . . doubt it . . . fuckers . . ."

Wayne blinked back tears. "Steve—"

"Mean it, bro." More weak laughter. "Seeing Melissa spit in Cheney's face . . . shit . . . I know I did a . . . good . . . thing . . ."

"We love you, Steve." Melissa again, voice more clearly fraught with emotion now.

Steve shivered and coughed, then looked at Wayne through rheumy eyes. "I love you fuckers, too. And Wayne . . . every time I call you bro . . . I mean it . . . you're like a . . . brother to me." The weakest laugh yet. "That . . . don't make me a pussy . . . does it?"

Wayne wiped at his eyes. "Hell no."

He put the Cherokee in gear and drove away from the SIMRC. He glanced at the rearview mirror and watched the burning building disappear from view. Steve fell silent as they traveled a maze of winding back roads. He spoke up again as they neared a residential subdivision, a shabby patch of land packed with tiny prefab homes. Wayne parked at the curb outside one of the houses and they sat there for a time, watching the dark sky turn slowly to gray. Dawn and the beginning of a new day. At one point Steve roused himself from yet another death-like slumber and made a music request. Wayne shuffled through the tapes in the glove compartment and found Van Halen's *Women And Children First*. He fast-forwarded to the song "Fools" and turned the volume up a bit.

Steve grinned and mouthed the words to the song.

He looked at Wayne as the song neared its end and said, "Listen to that guitar. No one shreds like EVH. Had to . . . hear that . . . one more time. That's the sound . . . of . . ."

He didn't say anything else.

Twenty One
Mama, I'm Coming Home

Carol Wade was still asleep and dreaming as dawn broke that day. The dream was the good kind. Some hot and muscular stud between her legs, grinding away at her goods, filling her up with a dick that felt bigger than the largest dildo in her impressive personal collection of sex toys. Then something intruded on the dream, a distant sound like the whisper of wind chimes on a cool evening breeze. The sound came again and the vision of the hunk's glistening torso dissipated as she rose against her will toward consciousness.

She awoke to find herself tangled in sweaty bedsheets. One of the young men renting the house next to hers was in bed beside her. He looked nothing like the hunk of her dream. He was scrawny, with a pale, sunken chest. He had thin, wormy lips and buck teeth. A faint wisp of a mustache and gaunt cheeks dotted with acne scars. His stomach hitched as she watched him sleep and he made a loud honking sound in his throat.

Carol grimaced.

Robert Redford this boy ain't.

Hell, he was a nerd. Albeit one grown into his twenties and working in the computer business in some way. Which just made him more of a loser in Carol's eyes. Anyone could see there was no future in tinkering with stupid gadgets. The boy could have a cushy job in the factory where she worked. She'd been willing to put in a good word for him, but he'd spurned the offer. Sometimes she got the feeling he thought he was better than her, that he was only with her for the easy pussy. Getting his dick wet on a regular basis for the first time in his nerd life, gaining experience that would benefit him

112

when the time came to move on to something better.

Thinking about it stirred a familiar anger, a bitter resentment that was always there. Carol couldn't stand the idea of anyone thinking they were better than her. Sometimes she obsessed about it, especially when she didn't have some dim boy around to fuck senseless. The ones she devirginized even sort of worshiped her for a while. But even they would inevitably turn against her. Carol could never figure it out. Seemed everyone she met eventually formed the same opinion about her. That she was trashy. Not fit to mix with decent folk. Well, fuck them.

She watched the boy's open mouth as he snored.

Even this one, pathetic as he was, would start avoiding her soon if the pattern held true.

She imagined tipping a spoonful of rat poison down that gaping mouth.

Yeah, she thought. *Poison your nerd ass.*

Let's see you look down on me then, cocksucker.

Carol gave the murderous notion serious thought. She had never killed anyone on purpose. That hit and run thing years ago had been an accident. Some geezer out walking his little dog at three in the morning got clipped by her Impala. Dumb old man should have known to be looking for drunk drivers. His fault. She still liked to look at her newspaper clippings about the incident now and then, deriving a dark little thrill from the hazy memories every time. How much more exciting would it be to off someone on purpose? She could do it. She thought of the big jar of rat poison beneath the kitchen sink and made up her mind.

This is gonna be fun.

She smiled.

Yeah, there'd be the matter of what to do with the body and explaining things to the cops after Poindexter's roommates reported him missing, but—

The doorbell rang.

And not for the first time, she realized. She was sure the sound was what had pulled her out of the delicious dream. A glance at the digital clock on her nightstand showed it was barely after 5 am, way too early for anyone who didn't want her foot up their ass to be ringing her bell.

The bell chimed again and she grumbled a curse. She swung her legs over the side of the bed, found the nerd's big button-up shirt among a pile of discarded clothes on the floor, and shrugged it on as she stood up and stalked out of the room. She flicked on a light as she entered the hallway, then another as she passed through an archway into the small living room.

"Dear God . . ." she groaned.

The living room was a disaster. An open pizza box on the floor. Cats nibbling on leftover slices. A wide array of empty liquor and beer bottles clogged every available surface. There were more bottles and cans on the floor. The musky scent of sex was just detectable through the entrenched tobacco odor. The sofa was pushed back from the coffee table. Pillows were on the floor. She vaguely remembered getting fucked doggy style by nerdo in here before taking the party to the bedroom. Hard to remember for sure, what with all the fuckin' drinking they'd done. That and the groovy pills.

The sound of an engine idling somewhere outside her house made her frown. She kicked her way through a cluster of empty and crushed Schaefer Light cans, circumvented the sofa, and arrived at the window that overlooked her front yard. She pulled back the drapes and saw a green Jeep Cherokee parked at her curb. It was still half-dark out but she was able to make out two murky shapes in the vehicle. She didn't recognize the car.

Who the fuck?

The doorbell rang again.

Enough of this bullshit.

She turned from the window and strode rapidly toward the door. She almost felt sorry for the asshole. Anyone stupid enough to wake her at so ungodly an hour on a fucking Saturday deserved the beating they were about to take. She yanked the front door open and an expletive died in her throat.

The Jeep Cherokee's engine revved and a moment later it sped away from the curb. The driver hooked a left at the nearest side street and was gone.

Carol barely noticed.

Her son was standing on her porch, swaying on his feet, head hung down as he stared at her through glazed, empty eyes. She hadn't seen the boy in years, hadn't even seen a picture, but motherly instinct told her it was true. This was her boy, no doubt about it.

He didn't look too good. Not that she cared.

She recovered from the initial shock and slapped him hard across the face. The blow almost knocked him off his feet. "What're you doin' here, shithead? Get back home to your worthless daddy before I call the fuckin' cops. I don't want you on my property."

He just stared at her and made an odd hissing sound.

She frowned. "The fuck's wrong with you? You turn out retarded or somethin'?" Her face went bright red with rage. "Your daddy better not think he can push your mushbrain ass off on me. I'll put you on a bus right back to . . ."

Carol's frown deepened.

She'd noticed the blood dripping from the boy's bandaged forearm. Droplets intermittently spattered the painted concrete porch.

She took a closer look at his pale face then and felt the first real flicker of fear.

Too late.

Steve Wade snarled and pulled his mother close.

Carol Wade screamed as her son's teeth punctured her flesh.

Her last sight as a living creature was the ravening hunger in his dead eyes.

Epilogue
Messianic Reprise

USA TODAY HEADLINE, NOV. 21, 1987

HUNDREDS DEAD IN ILLINOIS
FEDS DECLARE ZOMBIE 'PANIC' CONTAINED

Wayne and Melissa fled west to California, arriving in the so-called City of Angels several weeks after the SIMRC burned. Too much had happened to even consider returning to their former lives. Melissa couldn't stomach the idea of returning to her intolerant stepfather and mother, and Wayne was unable to bear the prospect of facing his father after all he'd done. They supported themselves with various menial jobs along the way.

Melissa realized she was pregnant long before they arrived in Los Angeles.

"Our hearts go out to the families of the dead in Illinois. We can take comfort in knowing that the departed have ascended to a better place and are suffering no more. And I pledge that my administration will do everything in its power to identify the culprit behind this heinous attack on our nation's heartland."

—President Ronald in his address to the nation on Nov. 22, 1987

Melissa and Wayne started having sex weeks prior to their arrival in California, but Melissa knew the timing was all wrong. Mark Cheney's malignant seed had planted the life growing inside her.

116

And though this sickened her, she couldn't bring herself to abort that life. The baby was born and put up for adoption. Through sheer coincidence, its adoptive parents soon moved to Illinois and Melissa's child grew up within a few miles of her own childhood stomping grounds.

The child's name was Melinda, and her childhood was even more troubled than Melissa's had been. Her adoptive parents divorced and she was shuttled through a succession of distant relatives, including an aunt who eventually sent her to Tennessee to live with cousins.

Melinda grew up to face zombie problems of her own.

"Did you hear the one about the Illinois zombies? No?"

(LONG PAUSE)

(PHOTO OF A STUNNED INFIELDER AFTER A BOTCHED PLAY IS FLASHED)

"You may know them better as the Chicago Cubs."

(POLITE LAUGHTER, SCATTERED APPLAUSE)

—Johnny Carson, from a Tonight Show monologue

Melissa and Wayne lived with a guilt so crushing their eventual descent into alcoholism and addiction had been inevitable. They had been fully aware, of course, of the second wave of zombie killings initiated by the impulsive act of dropping off their dying friend at his estranged mother's house. The tail-end of the 80's turned dark for them, the early 90's darker yet.

They eventually split and Wayne meandered through the next several years, spending his last months in a shabby apartment off the Sunset Strip, where he was stabbed to death while zoned out on heroin. His killer was never caught. No one cared, especially the police. Just another dead doper.

Melissa had started writing songs in the late 80's. Dark, brooding, angry songs. She formed a band and assumed lead vocal duties, working as a stripper on weekends to help pay for the band's gear. The band was a hit on the club circuit. After Nirvana hit and changed the musical landscape, things were wide open for artists like Melissa, who soon adopted the stage name "Nikki Taylor." Her band scored a major label deal, put out two albums, and had two minor radio hits, "Reform School Junkie" and a punk cover of "Because The Night." She lived comfortably off the royalties from these songs until her suicide in 1999.

A lengthy criminal investigation turned up evidence of vile crimes probably perpetrated by people in authority at the Southern Illinois Music Re-Education Center. Numerous indictments were handed down as public outrage soared.

The SIMRC was never rebuilt.

And rock and roll lives on.

About the Author

Bryan Smith is the author of several mass-market horror novels, including *Depraved*, *The Killing Kind*, *The Freakshow*, *Deathbringer*, *House of Blood*, *Queen of Blood*, and *Soultaker*. That's actually all of them released so far. No real need for use of the word "including", eh? But you know what? I'm gonna leave it in there because I am a rebel and you cannot fucking stop me. Go ahead. It's already in print. There is literally not a single goddamn thing you can do about it. Well...I suppose you could cross it out. Anyway. Bryan lives in middle Tennessee with his lovely wife Rachael Wise. Also, a lot of animals live with them, including the ferocious attack dogs Maggie and Molly (See! Those names positively ring with ferocity). A couple of his books have been published in fancy-ass limited editions. He's done some other shit here and there, but why bother with minutiae? There's more stuff in the works. He has one of those website sort of things. You can check it out at www.bryansmith.info.

deadite press

"Brain Cheese Buffet" Edward Lee - collecting nine of Lee's most sought after tales of violence and body fluids. Featuring the Stoker nominated "Mr. Torso," the legendary gross-out piece "The Dritiphilist," the notorious "The McCrath Model SS40-C, Series S," and six more stories to test your gag reflex.

"Edward Lee's writing is fast and mean as a chain saw revved to full-tilt boogie."
- Jack Ketchum

"Bullet Through Your Face" Edward Lee - No writer is more extreme, perverted, or gross than Edward Lee. His world is one of psychopathic redneck rapists, sex addicted demons, and semen stealing aliens. Brace yourself, the king of splatterspunk is guaranteed to shock, offend, and make you laugh until you vomit.
"Lee pulls no punches."
- Fangoria

"The Innswich Horror" Edward Lee - In July, 1939, antiquarian and H.P. Lovecraft aficionado, Foster Morley, takes a scenic bus tour through northern Massachusetts and finds Innswich Point. There far too many similarities between this fishing village and the fictional town of Lovecraft's masterpiece, The Shadow Over Innsmouth. Join splatter king Edward Lee for a private tour of Innswich Point - a town founded on perversion, torture, and abominations from the sea.

"Slaughterhouse High" Robert Devereaux - It's prom night in the Demented States of America. A place where schools are built with secret passageways, rebellious teens get zippers installed in their mouths and genitals, and once a year one couple is slaughtered and the bits of their bodies are kept as souvenirs. But something's gone terribly wrong when the secret killer starts claiming a far higher body count than usual . . .
"A major talent!" - Poppy Z. Brite

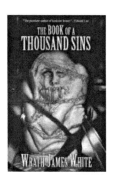

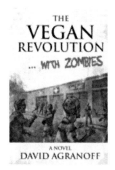

LaVergne, TN USA
11 February 2011
216025LV00005B/100/P